LOVE ME, LORD TENDER

DEB MARLOWE

A Series of Unconventional Courtships

Love Me, Lord Tender
Nothing But a Rakehell
and
coming soon
Kiss Me, Lady, One More Time

CHAPTER 1

A little bird has whispered in my ear. The reclusive Lord Terror has arrived in Town. Guard the women in your families, gentlemen. Rumor has it that Lord Terror does not always display the respect that is due a lady...

--Whispers From Lady X

LADY HOPE BRIGHTLEY weaved skillfully through the throng at Lady Loxton's ball. She was following her nose toward the buffet, until her sister-in-law grabbed her and pulled her behind a potted plant.

"Just where do you think you are going?" Catherine, Lady Kincade, hissed.

Hope rubbed her wrist. "To the buffet," she answered absently. "I rather fancy the sound of the lobster patties."

"Lobster patties! Lobster patties? How can you be thinking of lobster patties *now*? Lord Bardham has just left me and he is most upset! He says that you have treated him quite coldly."

"I am not surprised that he would say so." Hope craned

her neck toward the food, hoping her sister-in-law would get the hint. "I refused his offer. He didn't take it well." She took a step away. "I shall speak with you later, Catherine."

But Catherine grabbed her again. "*Refused* him? Why? Why would you be so foolish?"

"I do not care for him—as I have told you before."

"He is a fine young man, my brother's closest friend. What possible objection could you have?"

"He is younger than I, for one. And as I have told you, I find him insincere."

Catherine waved both of those objections off. "The age difference means nothing. And as I said, every suitor has a few honeyed words—"

"Honeyed is one thing. Salacious is another." Hope shivered. "His words, his insinuating looks, the way he acts as if I were as good as betrothed to him already, just because he has shown an interest—it's all feels more slimy than honeyed. No. I do not care for him." Hope speared the tiresome woman with a stern look. "And if you are the one who is encouraging him in his suit, then I beg you to stop."

Catherine reared back. "Oh? And whom should I encourage? It's not as if you are entertaining a host of suitors, all ready to go down on one knee. And at your age, the chances that such a thing would occur . . ."

She allowed her words to trail off into dire, silent speculation.

Hope sighed. "The Season has barely begun. As you point out—again—I have waited overlong to enjoy it. But enjoy it, I mean to do." She nodded over Catherine's shoulder. "Your brother approaches." Hope suspected that both Catherine and her brother, Mr. James Judson, were behind Lord Bardham's persistent and unwelcome attentions. "I imagine you wish to share the bad news."

She left her sister-in-law sputtering, determined to make

her escape. She tried to make allowances for the woman. Her own brother implored her to do so often enough, trying to keep the peace between his wife and sister. But Catherine was so irritating. She'd been trying to get rid of Hope since Papa had passed on and Matthew had inherited the title. Certainly, she'd made it easier to contemplate moving on.

But if Hope was going to leave her younger sister, her home, and everything and everyone she loved, well then, she was going to do it on her own terms.

Right now, though, she was going to enjoy a lobster patty. Or two.

* * *

WILLIAM GREY, Lord Tensford, eyed his host from across the room and suppressed a sigh of impatience. He could not recall when he'd last attended a London ball. All around him, members of the *ton* eyed him askance. Some gave awkward nods or the occasional bow. Others frowned or let their gazes slide away as if they had not been staring.

They looked at him with knowing eyes, as if they were already acquainted with everything about him.

They were not. Nor did they care to be, he had found. They were not interested in Will Grey. Only in the terrible Earl of Tensford.

He hated hearing his name whispered as he passed. He despised hearing his nickname even more. Lord Terror. Ridiculous.

He refused to let their disdain affect him. But he hated being the object of their gossip.

He moved on. He'd been waiting to speak with the host of

this evening's event. A chance for a word with Lord Loxton had been the only thing to tempt him here this evening. But the earl had been huddled in a corner with Lord Kincade for quite a while. He wondered if they discussed the growing unrest in the country. It was part of the reason why he was here. Loxton, he had heard, was rumored to have had quite a bit of success in modernizing his estates and keeping his tenants happy despite the current difficulties.

Tensford would be thrilled to glean any bit of advice in that direction. It would be the height of bad manners to interrupt, however. So he wandered, impatient with the delay.

A pair of young ladies breezed past him. So caught up were they, in their giggling behind their fans, that they failed to watch their step. A risk in a crowd like this. And sure enough, as one girl leaned in to whisper, she stepped on her friend's hem, sending her stumbling.

"Whoops!" Tensford reached out and caught the young lady, setting her back on her feet. "There you are."

Eyes twinkling, she looked up. "Oh, thank you so—"

She stopped. All of her bright color drained away. "Oh!" She looked as if she might fall over again—into a faint. "Lord Terror!"

Her friend snatched her close. "Lord Tensford, thank you for catching Dolly. It's so close in here, she might have been stepped on." She retreated, dragging her friend with her. "Do excuse us."

The girl he'd caught stared back at him as they fled, all of her laughter and exuberance drowned in fear. Fear of what? Of him? Of taint? Of scandal?

Fury churned like lava in his gut. He suffered the irresistible urge to do something. Something wicked. Whisper a naughty invitation to a starchy matron or snap his teeth and growl like a dog at a wide-eyed debutante. Why not? If he was going to be condemned without trial or question, then he might as well earn his fiendish reputation.

He paced a while longer, ignoring the crowd and keeping an eye on his host, waiting to catch him alone. After a few minutes, he considered leaving and catching the man another time.

But a footman passed with a tray of canapés, intent on replenishing the buffet. Tensford's stomach growled. So, instead, he followed in the servant's wake.

Tarts. That's what the footman carried to the end of the buffet. He set about arranging them, while Will took up a plate and the last lobster patty and then turned to the platter of cheeses.

"Oh, dear." A feminine voice sounded close behind him. He glanced back to see a woman moving away from him, approaching the footman. "Will it be a long delay?" she asked. "Before the lobster patties are replenished? I heard Lady Arthnaught say they were culinary creations of sheer bliss."

Color drained from the servant's face. "I'm very sorry, miss," he said in a hushed tone. "But the kitchen has run short of lobster patties."

"Oh, dear. How disappointing."

"But the cook is preparing a lovely salmon mousse," he offered.

"Thank you." She turned back to peruse the other choices and gave Tensford a glancing smile.

He blinked. Before it could bloom as a conscious thought in his head, Tensford stepped forward, offering his plate. "But of course, if this is the last, then you must have it."

It was because of her easy smile. And because of her eyes. Large and shining and the same deep, warm brown as his mother's sable coat, they sparkled up at him over a nose that was long and snubbed the smallest bit at the end. Her hair was sleek and a similar rich, chocolate color. It contrasted wonderfully with the soft yellow of her gown.

Their gazes held. She reached for the plate, all comfortable manner and pleasant acceptance.

And his stomach let out a long, gurgling protest.

The footman's laugh turned into a cough as he quickly fled. And then it came—the assessing gaze, the measuring look that would size him up and reduce him to pound notes, parliamentary votes, and rumors of his callous disregard of his family.

He stiffened. Drew the haughty veil of his indifference around him.

Except that the assessment looked different on her. Kinder. Her gaze touched on his suddenly fisted hand, on the tense set of his shoulders. It lingered on the faint shadows that he knew lived beneath his eyes.

"You are very kind, sir," she said softly. "But I think perhaps you need that small bit of bliss more than I."

With a nod, she turned away.

He stood, transfixed. Something momentous had just happened. Hadn't it?

"Perhaps we might share," he blurted after her.

She turned and looked back. "The lobster patty?" she asked carefully.

"Or the bliss," he breathed. "If you prefer."

She took a step closer. "I do think that would be frowned upon."

He laughed bitterly. "So many things are."

She considered him for a moment. "True. All the really interesting things."

"It does seem so." He held out the plate again. "Perhaps we might start with the lobster and move on from there?"

"Into more interesting territory?" she whispered. "It sounds dangerous."

"We could start with canapés. Or perhaps a dance. If more dangerous territory was to follow . . ." He shrugged.

Her big, bright eyes unfocused a little, as if she was imagining it.

"Lady Hope Brightley?" Another footman had approached. "Lord Kincade requests your presence in the library."

She shook her head as if to clear it. "Ah. Perhaps my brother is ready to depart. You see?" She smiled at Tensford. "The last lobster patty was meant for you. You enjoy it. I'll let my brother's kitchens feed me, once we're home."

She walked away, following in the footman's wake. He stared after her, still a little befuddled.

But then he frowned. She was Kincade's sister? He glanced toward the other side of the ballroom, where he thought he could just see the man through the crush, still conversing with their host.

He closed his eyes. Despite his earlier temptation, the last thing he needed was to embroil himself in . . . anything. The damned *beau monde* had had enough entertainment at his expense.

He should let it go. He should.

Setting down the plate, he followed after her.

* * *

IT WAS ONLY as she was crossing the room that she heard someone's remark and realized who he was.

Lord Tensford. The infamous Lord Terror.

Not so terrible in her estimation. Gracious, but he was handsome. Tall enough to look up to, but without being overbearing. Dark hair, tousled just the most tempting bit, making a girl wish to smooth it. A square jaw, a straight Roman blade of a nose—and the most striking light green eyes, like none she'd ever seen. She'd been quite caught up in his gaze, comfortably amused with his banter, and somewhat enthralled with the sparkle that erupted into the air between them.

Why the horrible nickname, then? She could only recall vague rumors about his cavalier treatment of his family. She frowned. No care for anyone but himself. That was the whisper she remembered.

Surely it was an exaggeration? If anything, Hope had thought he'd looked careworn. As if something worried him and weighed upon him.

"Here we are, Miss." The footman opened a heavily carved door.

"Thank you."

The library was large, but only dimly lit.

"Matthew?" she called softly, stepping in.

The light grew dimmer still as the servant shut the door behind her. She ventured further. "If you've called me here to berate me over Bardham, then you are wasting your time. I will not have him."

"Oh, but you will."

She rounded a pillar and came face to face with her rejected suitor himself. "What are you doing?"

Lord Bardham was moving furniture, creating an open space before the long windows. With a grimace in her direction, he pulled cushions and pillows from the comfortable chairs and piled them on the floor. "I'm setting the scene." He said it as if it should have been plain.

Hope turned on her heel and headed back the way she'd come.

The door was locked.

Don't panic.

Catherine. Or her brother, James. It must be one of them, in cahoots with Bardham, trying to force her hand. She could pound on the door and shout, but she doubted she'd be heard over the noise of the ball—and she might be putting her foot straight into their trap.

"Come, now." Bardham was right behind her. "You've demonstrated your maidenly shyness. Now we move forward. I know you are not very . . . experienced in the world, but I can teach you what you need to know."

Her chin went up. "Lord Bardham, if you wish for a wife who finds such declarations romantic or even acceptable, then you must search elsewhere. I've already refused you once this evening. Do not make me do so again."

"There is no good reason to refuse me, my dear. In fact, it all fits perfectly. I have debts. You have a substantial dowry. And as a matchmaker's fee, my dear friend James has a place in my father's canal scheme. Everyone gets what they want, if only you cease to be stubborn."

"Everyone but me." She glared at him.

"Ah, but you get the best prize of all." He gave her a flourishing, little bow. "Me." Rising up, he grabbed her upper arms and pulled her in for a kiss.

She shook her right arm free and hit him in the nose.

She was too close to get enough leverage for a really good punch, but he let her go and grabbed at his nose as it began to bleed. "You spiteful bitch!"

He pushed her away from the door and toward his makeshift boudoir. She stumbled, but kept on going, stepping over to the pillows to the window and throwing up the sash. She was lifting her skirts and preparing to step out when he caught up and tried to grab her again.

She slapped his hand away. "Have you been drinking, sir?

You cannot believe that I would allow you to ravish me during the Loxton ball."

He laughed and wiped at his bloody nose. "I don't have to ravish you, I only need to make everyone believe that I did."

Fear and fury vied for dominance. "Perhaps I only need to make everyone believe you incapable of accosting me." For a moment she was angry enough to contemplate fighting back, but if they were discovered . . .

No. She threw a leg out of the window. It was so long and wide, stepping out onto the terrace would be easy.

But he caught a hold of her skirts. "I'm not letting you get away. I have plans for . . . you."

A step sounded behind her. Someone approached on the terrace. Caught in her awkward position, she could only see a dark figure step near.

"Is that you? You're too early, damn you." Bardham made a shooing motion with one hand. "Give me a few moments more, then come in through the door as planned."

"Unhand the lady. Now."

Bardham backed up, viciously yanking at her skirts and unbalancing her so that she fell back into the library. The man outside stepped close to peer in.

"Tensford?? Bardham sounded incredulous. "Stay out of this. It's none of your business."

Her head snapped up.

"Still making a nuisance of yourself, Boredom? Some things never change. You need to find a new way to outrun that old nickname."

Bardham laughed, and then he reached down to haul Hope to her feet. "Run along, Lord Terror, and I shall endeavor to live up to *your* nickname, once you've gone."

Even in the dim light, the furious flush of color in the earl's face was obvious. He stepped inside, clearing the window without a hint of effort. "I tell you again, let her go—

or I will hold you down and allow her to do as she threatened. The lady looks furious. I expect she'll kick you in the stones so hard, your grandchildren will feel it."

"Get out!" Bardham had begun to sound unhinged. "The girl is my intended. Leave her to me and confine your abuses to your own women."

Lord Tensford had no problem with leverage. He hauled back and planted Bardham a facer that sent him reeling back. The man tottered a moment, then crumpled to the floor.

"Are you all right?" Tensford's tone was still harsh, but his touch was gentle as he steered Hope away.

The fear and anger began to drain, leaving her shaking. She nodded up at him, blinking furiously as her eyes began to fill.

"Oh, no!" he said. "No tears. We are not done yet. Come." He held out a hand and she stared at it, finding it a welcome change from all the grabbing of her person that had gone on this evening. "Hurry. We cannot let you be found here."

She put her hand in his—and couldn't contain the shiver that went through her. He paused, looking for a moment at their clasped hands, then at her, before leading her to the window and helping her to climb through. Following, he tucked her hand in his arm and led her away. They strolled toward the wider portion of the terrace as if they'd only been following the curve of the balustrade.

"Are you betrothed to him?" he asked sharply.

"No." She shivered, but indignation began to rise again. "He offered. I refused. With no hesitation and utmost certainty."

"Ah." Some of the tension left the arm beneath her hand. "What is the man thinking?"

She snorted. "He is thinking of paying off his debts with my dowry, I believe."

"Then he must be deep in dun territory. This reeks of desperation."

"I don't know how to thank you." Pained, she paused. "We have not even been introduced. But you are Lord Tensford? I am Lady Hope Brightley—and I am so grateful."

"Don't be in such a hurry to thank me. We are not out of the woods yet," he said sardonically. "If you are going to emerge from this unscathed, there must not be a whisper of your involvement. It would be best if we got you to a public spot where you can appear calm and unruffled and then completely surprised if news of Bardham's condition becomes known."

"I know you must be right, but it infuriates me." She breathed out a huff of frustration. "I want to shout Bardham's perfidy from the rooftops, let everyone know exactly what he is—if only to prevent some other girl from falling into his clutches."

He stopped. "That is exactly what you must *not* do." It emerged on a severe note. An order. "You cannot give these people . . . anything." He waved at the house, shining and full to the brim with guests, his expression bitter. "Don't give them a morsel, a tidbit or even a whisper of scandal. It will not matter that Bardham is a fool and a predator. The truth will not matter. They will take the facts and twist and turn them to suit themselves, sculpting a scandal that fits their prejudices and appetites, spreading it and allowing it to grow until it no longer resembles even a particle of the truth."

They had reached the area of the terrace that lay outside the ballroom. The light from inside set his oddly lovely eyes to glittering. "Your innocence will be inconsequential. The fact that you acted just as you ought—it doesn't make a good enough story." He snorted. "The *ton* will delight in your downfall. Especially the women." His eyes rolled. "The fairer sex? That is a joke. You will hear them say things of you that you will scarcely believe."

She stared up at him and wondered if he knew how he was exposing his own pain. "Is that what happened to you, my lord?"

He started, pulled back. For a moment, she thought that he wouldn't answer. She held her breath, afraid he would walk away.

He didn't. He glared again at the dancers whirling inside, at the people chatting and laughing. Then he looked back at her. "Thank you."

She blinked. "For .. ?"

"For asking. You are the first person who ever asked me."

The undeniable sadness of that statement struck her hard. Was he so alone?

"Yes," he answered. "That is exactly what happened to me." He took her arm and started them moving again. "It will not happen to you."

He paused and leaned against the rail next to the stairs and gestured below, over the small garden. "Do you see anyone you know? It would be best if you were among friends when Bardham awakes or his conspirator shows up."

She peered down. "Yes. There. I am acquainted with Miss Nichols."

"Perfect. We'll see you added to her group." He straightened and offered his arm again at the top of the stairway, but before she could take it, someone blurred past her and barreled into him, knocking him down the stairs."

"Oh, pardon." Sarcasm weighted the words. "I must have missed you there, Tensford."

"Lord Bardham, have you lost your senses?" She shrank back as the man turned to her. His cheek was split and bleeding, and his nose still trickled blood too. One eye was rapidly swelling and the other looked . . . utterly mad. "You should have cooperated," he growled.

"The lady refused you." Lord Tensford had managed to keep his feet. "Take your rejection like a gentleman," he growled.

"No." Bardham glared at her. "I don't believe I will."

"Heavens!" Miss Nichols and her friends had rushed forward. "What's happened?" She climbed the stairs to stand next to Hope.

Lord Tensford climbed after her. "Leave the girl alone," he told Bardham in a menacing tone. He turned then, and bowed to Hope. "It was a pleasure, Lady Hope." With nods to the gathering guests, he turned and stalked into the house.

Bardham whirled and went back the way he'd come.

"Gracious," someone murmured.

"What was that about?" another one asked.

"Are you well, Lady Hope?" Miss Nichols looked concerned.

"I'm fine, thank you." She was looking off after Tensford.

"What happened to Lord Bardham?"

She hesitated. "An accident?" she offered. "What else could it have been?"

The murmurs hiked up a notch.

"And Lord Terror? Did he mistreat you?" someone asked.

"No!" She looked around, determined that Tensford should not be subjected to further disparaging rumors because of her. "Lord Bardham seems quite . . . not himself this evening. But Lord Tensford was nothing but kind."

"Hard to believe that," someone said nastily.

"Please do believe it, nonetheless," she insisted, raising her voice so that all could hear her. "I only just met Lord Tensford this evening, but he treated me very kindly indeed. Almost tenderly," she added, in a whisper, to herself.

Someone laughed.

"Don't tease her." Miss Nichols put her arm around Hope. "Come, let's go and get you a glass of wine."

She nodded and let herself be taken in by the considerate girl. And though she watched carefully for the rest of the evening, she did not see the Earl of Tensford again.

CHAPTER 2

My dearest readers, it is true. Even Lady X can make a mistake. And it does seem that I, and indeed all of London, have been mistaken in Lord Terror. He attended the Loxton ball and was seen aiding not one, but two damsels in distress! At first I thought it a trick, but having heard the stories, I am convinced. Indeed, it seems we must change his moniker, dear readers. He is Lord Terror to us no longer, but, borrowing the words of one of the lucky damsels, we dub him our Lord Tender!

--Whispers from Lady X

TENSFORD BREATHED DEEPLY as he looked up from his accounts. Something smelled good. He felt hungry, really hungry, for the first time in a long while. Surprising, considering the state of the numbers he was working on, and the fact that he was no closer to solving his real dilemma.

But not so surprising, perhaps, since he felt the first glimmer of a lighter mood in months—and it had been brought to him along with a smile in a pair of dark, shining eyes.

He stood, stretching, as Higgins, his butler, entered with a tray. "Tea, sir. And Mrs. Agnew sends you some scones. They are not ginger cookies, alas."

"Ah, but ginger is pricey these days, Higgins, or so I hear."

"Yes, but they are your favorites, my lord. And you are the earl."

"We make do. And these smell good, too." He raised a brow at the man. "And we are lucky men, in the end. A good woman who is also a good cook? Mrs. Agnew is worth her weight in gold."

"I know you are correct, sir." The butler's expression changed but a moment. "Mrs. Agnew knows it, too."

Tensford grinned into his tea. His butler and cook shared a tumultuous relationship that kept the rest of the staff on their toes.

Higgins left and Tensford took up one of his ledgers.

He was going to have to reach a decision soon. Greystone Park needed an influx of cash. He'd done what he could with economies, with reorganization, and with the strict enforcement of budgets that had so upset his assorted female relatives.

He had spared no one, not even himself. To the horror of his mother, he had let the manor house at Greystone, leasing it for a year to an extremely wealthy merchant who wished to introduce his family to the social niceties of the gentry's country life before he took them up to Town. The servants had all stayed on and Tensford had moved himself into an empty tenant's cottage.

Even that had not been enough. Especially as the harvest was in danger this year, after such a disastrously wet and gloomy spring. It was hard enough keeping his people fed. How would he do it if they had a bad season?

He picked up the round, fist sized rock on his desk. Absently, his fingers traced the outline of the fossilized sea urchin that stretched over the curve of it. He'd found it on an expedition with his father. Fossil hunting had been the hobby they shared when he was a boy. It was still his hobby, in point of fact. It was peaceful. Quiet. His best hours were spent away at the riverside cliffs at Greystone, exploring the rocks, looking for signs of ancient life, caught forever.

When he'd first inherited and learned of the difficulties his estates were facing after years of his mother's stewardship, he'd hoped that his fossils might be their salvation. Good specimens fetched decent money. If he could find something really unusual, something large and intact, or something never seen before, it could bring in a fortune.

But he'd looked. Every spare minute, when he wasn't working at the estate, but he'd had to conclude that nothing valuable enough was to be found. He had to find another way.

He'd had an idea that he was developing with his steward. Much of Greystone Park's vast acreage was wooded. He could sell the timber. And if he set up his own mill and milled the lumber himself, he'd make an even higher profit. And he could mill for others in the region, as well. It was an expensive undertaking, however. Those giant blades were expensive and Gibbs, his steward, talked of a steam engine to run it—he could only imagine the cost of that.

He really did not wish to denude the ancient forests on his property. But he could not deny his need for cash.

The door opened again and Higgins stepped inside. "Lady Forsham has arrived, my lord."

His sister pushed her way into the room before Tensford could do anything save grimace.

"Good afternoon, Tensford."

"Fanny."

"Oh, good." Spotting the tray, she seated herself next to it. "Send up a fresh pot, won't you, Higgins?" She made a shooing motion with her hands. "Thank you."

Tensford sighed as Higgins shut the door with rather more force than was necessary. "Do refrain from ordering my servants about, please, Fanny?"

"Oh, posh! This is my home, too."

"It *was* your home, sister dear. You are Forsham's problem now."

"Do stop funning, William. I am here on serious business."

He already knew what sort of business.

"I need a small loan."

He mouthed the words at the same time as she spoke them.

"Oh, do stop! Why are brothers always so loathsome? I am utterly serious. I don't need much. Nothing above five or six hundred pounds, I shouldn't expect. I simply must redecorate the front parlor. It's still in the *Egyptian* style, William! Dreadfully out of date and so humiliating!"

Tensford pinched the bridge of his nose. "Let me explain to you again how this works, Fanny. You are *Forsham's* wife. If you wish to redo *Forsham's* parlor, then you must use *Forsham's* money."

"He doesn't have it," she said bluntly.

"Then how does this qualify as a loan?" he demanded.

"Oh, he'll have it eventually. He's due for a turn-around of luck. Even he cannot lose all of the time."

"Well, there you have it. Redecorate when your husband's luck turns."

"Oh, no. He has a long list of creditors panting after him. I cannot wait until he pays them all off."

"Neither can I."

"Oh, posh. Mother always managed to find money for me

when I needed it. It's not easy keeping to the forefront of fashion, brother."

"It's Mother's mismanagement of the family money that has put us all in these straits. Don't quote her mistakes to me."

She huffed in disapproval, but paused to look over the scones. Choosing one, she eyed him closely, clearly deciding to change tactics. "William, dear, you know you'll have plenty of money soon enough," she said in a wheedling tone. "And I must have the parlor done in Indian fashion. It's about to be all of the rage, I just know it. I have visions, William! Elephants and golden figures of Buddha and palm fronds and brilliant embroidery! Don't you *wish* to be sister to the leader of fashion in the *ton*?"

Plenty of money soon enough. He knew to what she referred. The time-honored tradition of an impoverished peer. She and his mother and aunt were waiting for him to marry for money.

She was still talking, but he'd quit listening. "Fanny," he interrupted. "If you and Mother and Aunt Camille are so eager for me to marry a fortune, then perhaps you should not have spread the rumors that make it an impossibility! Thanks to the three of you, the women of the *ton* wish nothing to do with me."

"I—spread rumors? Mother and I?" She took up her cup and raised her brow over it. "If you must blame someone, blame that meddlesome Lady X. She's the one who stuck you with that loathsome nickname."

"Oh, I know exactly who to blame." All the women in his family and Lady X, too. And now he was expected to sacrifice his future to set it all to rights. He'd be damned if he would.

"In any case," his sister continued. "There are other women, brother dear."

"I'll not be marrying that merchant's daughter that Mother keeps pushing at me," he declared. "She sat in the parlor at the dower house, estimated the cost of every stick of furniture and painting on the wall and gave me a rough number of the worth of the furnishings before she'd finished her first cup of tea."

"No, that one is unacceptable, I agree. But I introduced you to Miss Vouchell. Her father is a banker. She has quite a sizeable dowry and a biddable nature."

"Are you so sure of that?" He sat back and raised a brow at her. "I'm surprised to hear you push the match, sister. I heard her tell her mama that the first thing she means to do when she marries is to set up a receiving room in the Indian fashion."

His sister's teacup clattered into the saucer. "No! The little baggage! She wouldn't have the faintest notion of Indian decor without my guidance. Well." She straightened. "We will find you someone."

The door opened once more. "Mr. Sterne has arrived, my lord," Higgins intoned.

Tensford stood. "Barrett!" He left his desk to greet his old friend.

"You made it," Sterne grinned. "I know you said you were coming for the Season, but I didn't quite believe it. You sounded too utterly happy to be at home last year, with your estate improvements and your fossils. I was afraid you would succumb to their peaceful lure again."

Sterne was a man of science as well. He had come out to Greystone several times to hunt fossils, although he was not as much as an enthusiast as Tensford. His uncle, however, was one of the foremost experts in the field.

At his jest, Tensford cast a jaundiced eye to his sister. "I begin to wish I had."

His friend followed his gaze. "Oh, good morning to you, Lady Forsham. I hope you are well."

"Well enough." Fanny stood. "And better after Tensford and I settle this small matter."

"I'm sorry, Fanny." Tensford shook his head. "There are too many needs at Greystone. I have to rank hungry tenants higher than your elephants."

"Hmmph." Fanny's nose went into the air. "I should have known better than to ask. I told Forsham that this *tender* business was stuff and nonsense. He doesn't know you as I do." She swept toward the door. "Good day, Tensford. And I hope you feel it keenly when you enter some other hostess's parlor and find tiger skins and embroidered floor cushions."

"I'm sure I shall." But not for the reason she expected.

"Elephants?" Sterne asked as the door closed behind her. "Tiger skins?"

Tensford shook his head. "Just another fashion emergency." But he gazed after his sister. What did she mean when she mentioned *this tender business?*

"Well, we've no time for nonsense," Sterne said. "Come, and get rigged up. We're going out."

"Where?"

"Hadn't you heard? My uncle is giving a lecture at the Surrey Institution. This afternoon." He paused dramatically. "He's displaying some of the pieces from his collection?"

Tensford brightened. "The skull?"

"Of course."

He'd never seen it in person, the four-foot reptilian skull that had made Mr. John Sterne's name in naturalist circles. "Let's go, then."

In minutes, they were headed out. Sterne's driver had been walking the horses around Portman Square. They were turning the curved corner now, and the Tensford and Sterne stood talking as they waited on the pavement.

"I know you stayed away last Season because you felt like time and distance would allow the rumors around your name to fade. Have you put it to the test yet, this year?" Sterne asked.

Tensford sighed. "I did. At the Loxton ball, last night." Shaking his head, he admitted, "But it was all still turned shoulders, disapproving glares and young girls quaking in their shoes at the thought of exchanging a word with me."

"I did wonder," his friend said sympathetically. "There was as much talk when you were gone as when you were here."

"Spurned on by my female relatives, no doubt. They each love to play the martyr, and constantly try to outdo the others." Tensford hesitated. "However, there was one young lady, last night . . ."

"Oh?"

"She took the risk to converse with me. Spoke readily and easily. Even before—"

"Oh, watch now." Sterne stepped back and tipped his hat as a trio of young ladies approached, trailed by their maid.

Tensford moved quickly out of the way, wishing to avoid either glares or shivers, but the oldest, first in line, a pretty girl with large, grey eyes, nodded politely. She met his gaze—and paused.

He tensed, waiting.

But she *smiled*. Nodded again and dropped a curtsy. "So nice to see you again, Lord Tensford," she said. "A beautiful day, isn't it?"

The other two girls bobbed in his direction as well, then they all sailed on, heading for Upper Seymour Street.

Sterne grinned as Tensford stared after them. "Well, perhaps you had the right of it, after all. Might this mean that the tide has turned?"

He stared after the retreating figures. "Damn, but I hope it does."

* * *

THE SURREY INSTITUTION WAS CROWDED. Sterne's connection with the speaker meant that they had good seats in the lecture hall. A fortunate thing, because even the gallery above was filled with gentlemen—and ladies, too—all eager to hear Mr. Sterne speak.

He was skilled at it. Tensford was not the only one absorbed in his lecture and excited over his displays. When the talk finished, most of the attendees lingered, eager to discuss the scholar's theories and expand upon their own.

And it quickly became apparent that Barrett Sterne might just perhaps have been correct about the turning tide of public opinion. As they made their way down the aisle, debating fine points with a few others and comparing fossil discovery stories, it appeared that more than one young lady not only didn't avoid him, but might actually have sought out his opinion.

He exchanged a relief-filled glance with Barrett.

But as they slowly moved toward the exit, his hopes began to fade as it became obvious that the gentlemen were treating him differently as well.

"We thought you might not still be interested in fossils," Mr. Finch said with a smirk. "Hunting and chipping them free is so difficult and stony fossils are so *hard*."

"My interest hasn't changed," he replied warily.

"You cannot blame us for wondering." Finch's friend Harding elbowed him. "It's perhaps too much for a man with your *tender* sensibilities."

The pair of them snickered and a couple of other gentlemen chuckled along with them.

There was that word again. *Tender.* A sinking feeling began to make him sweat.

"Don't listen to these jackanapes." Lady Hargrove, an older woman with a keen mind and a quick sense of humor, was well known in scientific circles. "I find the whole affair ridiculous, but at least this new label is an improvement over the old."

"Indeed, the fact that he's out in public at all today proves that Tensford has a hide tough as leather." Barrett's uncle had joined them. He gave Tensford an approving nod. "Proving the gossips wrong, as usual."

The gossips? "I'm afraid I don't understand the joke," he said. And he knew he wasn't going to like it when he did.

"Oh, dear heavens. The man hasn't seen it." Lady Hargrove fanned her face with her notepad.

Anger and the old frustration began to rise. They'd all made their way out of the lecture hall and into the entryway. He blinked in the light. "Seen what?" he demanded.

The older lady snapped her fingers. "Someone find a copy of that dratted paper. He deserves to know what he's up against."

"I have a copy."

Tensford froze as Lady Hope Brightley approached their group, moving against the flow of traffic heading for the door.

"And as the entire debacle is my fault, I've come to apologize." She met his gaze directly. "I went to your home, first, my lord. I'm afraid I convinced your butler to reveal your whereabouts."

Dread sitting heavy in his gut, he held out his hand.

She gave over a folded newspaper, open to the pertinent page. "I am sorry," she whispered.

He read it.

Such a small thing. Just a few short sentences to have so much power—the ability to shape a man's life.

He should be used to it. Used to the frustration and madness of being judged unfairly and found wanting without true cause. But the hope that had begun to grow today made it worse. The thoughts about this girl that had unfurled deep in his heart . . . He looked at her set expression, at the worry in those pretty, dark eyes—and fury erupted in his chest.

It wasn't her fault. Or his either. But his name was a byword again. More notoriety, but no more money. He glanced over at the sniggering men, watching for his reaction. Any remote chance at finding a girl like . . . He looked at Lady Hope.

Perhaps a wellborn girl or two might look more kindly upon him now, but convincing her family to accept his suit—well, he still had not a snowball's chance in hell.

He wanted to rage. At these fools around at them, at the fickle Lady X, at the petty, bored *ton*, at the whole damned world.

He thrust the paper back at her, not trusting himself to speak. Instead, he pushed past her and out the door, ignoring the calls, the questions from them all.

Setting out, he jammed his hat on his head. It was a long, damned way home from Southwark. Maybe he'd feel better by the time he got there.

But he doubted it.

CHAPTER 3

I confess, I am at times bewildered at the antics of the young bucks of our Society . . . Lady X deigns to remind you that there are far worthier activities than making fools of yourself for the sake of a betting book gamble . . . we beg of you -- go forth and find one, gentlemen!

--Whispers from Lady X

STRAIGHTENING HER GLOVES, Hope gazed across the crowded room. Mr. Jack Alden, young as he was, held a reputation as a noted scholar and a specialist in ancient cultures, but he was developing an interest in the natural sciences after the discovery of two tree-sized fossilized ferns at his family's Dorsetshire estate. A second son, he was using his brother's house to throw this party and had invited the scientific set to come and discuss the findings and view his etchings and notes.

Hope knew Tensford had been invited and suspected it would be an impossible evening to resist. She'd wangled an invitation to accompany Miss Nichols—who was invited everywhere—so that she could finally face Tensford and offer a proper apology.

And good heavens, she did owe him one. She hadn't been in Town when he'd been saddled with that first nickname. She scoffed at it now and would have then, no doubt, but if the hue and cry and attention had been anything like what he suffered now . . . she shuddered.

The young bucks of the *ton* were having a grand time amusing themselves at his expense.

"Yoo hoo, Lord Tender!" They waved and called and batted their eyes at him whenever he ventured beyond his door.

And the pranks . . . they were endless. One young wit hired a parade of women to knock at his door one day. One after the other, when the door opened, they all thrust a child forward. "The birch rod does no good with this one," they all proclaimed in one version or another. "P'raps Lord Tender's ways might reach him and show him how to go on."

Another bribed a butcher to pull a beef-laden cart to the earl's door. "Here's all my toughest cuts of meat," he bellowed loud enough to be heard all over Portman Square. "Lord Tender, help me out with 'em, won't you?"

Next a broadsheet had been plastered all over Town, depicting a risqué musical number being performed in a brothel—and being interrupted by the distraught bawd. *No, no!* she screeched in a bubble over her head. *You are all too coarse for this delicate piece! Somebody fetch Lord Tender! He'll show ye!*

Society's ladies were not much better. Half of them had declared that this latest was just a ruse on Tensford's part, to make everyone forget his true, terrible nature. The other half had decided that such acknowledged instances of gallantry showed promise and must be encouraged.

It was a disgrace, the way they all behaved—and it was all Hope's fault. The very least she could do was apologize.

But then she remembered the magnificent storm in his eyes when he'd read that gossip. And the night that they'd met and his slow, warm smile, the way her pulse had quickened at their banter and how the air between them had come alive . . .

And she knew that she wished to do more than the very least.

She feared it was too late.

But she meant to find out.

Stepping up next to Miss Nichols, she smiled as her friend took her arm. "He's here somewhere. I'd wager on it," she said.

Hope grinned. "Let's hunt him down, then, shall we?"

They found him in the parlor, talking with their host. Miss Nichols patted her hand and went on, but Hope lingered behind a curio cabinet, waiting for the pair's earnest discussion of rock layers to wind down.

Eventually, Mr. Alden was called away, and when Lord Tensford made to leave, she stepped right out into his path.

He stopped.

She ignored the jolt to her heart at his closeness. "I'm quite persistent," she warned.

"And determined, if I can correctly read the glint in your eye."

"I'm afraid so. Your wisest course would be to just allow me to have my say."

"Very well." He folded his arms. "Have at it."

She set her shoulders. "I do most humbly beg your pardon. That night—you saved me. You were most heroic. They tried to disparage you and I defended you. The last bit —about you acting tenderly—it was just a whisper, meant for no one but myself. But it was heard, and just look at the mischief it's caused you." She shook her head. "I am truly sorry."

"Forgiven." He straightened. "I must offer my regrets as well, for stalking off the first time you attempted your handsome apology. I couldn't trust myself not to vent my anger."

"I would have deserved it," she said humbly, and meaning it.

"You would not have. Neither of us is to blame in this. It is the *beau monde*."

"They are behaving badly." She sighed.

"The young bloods are vainglorious, overeager pups, without a care who is harmed by their fun. The ladies are as bad—empty-headed sheep, willing to follow anyone whistling the latest *on-dit*." He shrugged. "I suppose I should thank you, though. At least it's become fashionable with some of the ladies to encourage my reformation. There are more than a few now, who manage not to drop or run when I draw near."

"A small blessing," she murmured, feeling worse than ever.

"Not that any of their fathers will entertain an offer from a notorious, pockets-to-let fellow like me. But not to worry," he said ironically. "My mother and aunt both have bridal candidates they wish me to meet. And that will be my fate, in the end." The resignation in his tone set her heart to aching. "Some merchant's daughter or cit's girl will take me, and I'll be grateful enough, if it allows me to set things aright at Greystone."

"Oh, dear."

"But not quite yet," he said, becoming more animated. "First I mean to make the most of this Season."

Surely he was too young to have worry lines at the edges of his green eyes? And it was a certainty that she shouldn't be wishing to smooth them with a finger. "Looking for a girl with wits enough to see what a fine gentleman you are?"

"Lord, no. There's no use in wishful thinking. No." He

rubbed his hands together. "I mean to attend all the scientific events to be had, dance with a pretty girl or two, and finally . . ." He lowered his voice to a dramatic baritone. "I will unmask the mysterious Lady X."

That startled her. "Unmask Lady X? Do you think that wise?"

"Why not?"

"Because you may not find what you expect. Who knows why she writes her gossip? Perhaps she has a good reason."

"A good reason to interfere with the lives of others? No. She is a shepherdess with an acid pen and she's put it to use in altering the course of my life. Why should I not return the favor? Perhaps, in the process, I might even shake a few ladies of the *ton* awake. Who knows? They might even begin to think for themselves."

"You don't think much of women, do you, sir?"

"And should I? It was my own mother, sister and aunt who started all of this—all because I cut their profligate spending and forced them to tighten their belts like the rest of us at Greystone. One sent her story of my cruelty to her friends, and the other two were not to be outdone. Tales of my harsh, miserly ways and the horrors I subjected them to spread and caught the attention of Lady X. And thus my fate was sealed."

"But not all women are so short-sighted."

"True. I know more than a few good, kind and worthy women, but none of them are in the peerage. Society ladies are too often silly, shallow and short of both sense and intellect."

She took a step back. "I think you forget who you are speaking to, my lord. I am a lady of the peerage."

He merely grunted and rolled his eyes. "Well, present company excepted, of course. You don't think I would include you in such a list of deficiencies?"

"I think you easily could. You barely know me, after all."

"I know enough," he said gruffly.

She dipped her head. "I thank you for the compliment." Lowering her brow, she stared at him.

"What now? I think perhaps I know you well enough to be nervous at that look."

"I am getting an idea."

Now he truly looked alarmed.

"You're right," she said baldly. She was happy to see that he was smart enough not to relax. "It is a problem, is it not?"

He frowned. "Which? I've more than enough to choose from."

"The marriage mart." She waved a hand. "The whole process by which the *ton* contracts a marriage. Titles, money, political power—they are reason enough for some people to marry. Clearly, some are happy to choose using such criteria. But not all of us. Not you, I think, sir."

"And not you?"

"Definitely not me. I have different measures of a man. Is he kind? Responsible? Can he laugh at the absurdities of life? Does he have enough heart to feel the sorrows?"

He laughed. "Good luck finding such a paragon."

"He's out there," she said confidently. "There are good men. Just as there are good women in the peerage." She eyed him with speculation. "I daresay there is even one out there who would have you."

"Such a fairytale creature does not exist." He stopped, suddenly arrested. "Unless you happen to be a fabulously wealthy heiress?"

Disappointment gripped her, but she forced a laugh. "All the world knows that I am quite an eligible catch, despite my three and twenty years, my lord. I have a good family name and two thousand pounds set aside by my father for a respectable dowry."

He sighed in obvious disappointment. "Only two thousand? I need a good deal more to repair the damage my mother has wreaked in her years of stewardship." He grinned at her. "Couldn't you wangle more out of your brother?"

"Ha!" she scoffed. "Catherine has tight hold of those purse strings. And I've no more wish to be married for money than you do to be dismissed for lack of it."

"I can't blame you." He sighed. "But neither can I help but be disappointed." He smiled, but the heat in his gaze awoke a similar, slow burn in her belly. "I do think we'd get on well together," he said, his tone lower.

She shivered. "I believe there is hope for you yet." Chin raised, she looked him up and down. "Moreover, I am going to help you find the lady you seek."

Now he looked interested in a different way.

"Yes," she continued. The idea was firming, growing. "You did me a good turn, my lord. And I am going to return the favor, as you put it." She put a finger to her chin. "But how to go about it? It cannot be in the usual fashion, an introduction at a ball or Society event. How to show you a young lady's truly valuable qualities?" She narrowed her gaze, thinking.

"A scheme," he said admiringly. "You're getting one up, aren't you? I can see the wheels turning." He tilted his head. "I'll go along with yours if you go along with mine."

"Yours?"

"To unmask Lady X. Have you forgotten already?"

"Oh." Her heart fell. "I don't know. I don't think it is a good idea. People could be hurt. You could be one of them."

"Fine, then. I won't ask you to assist in the actual sleuthing. But I may request that you invite me along to a Society event or two that I might not be invited to, on my own."

She considered. "Very well." She extended her hand. "Shall we shake hands to mark the deal?"

He took her hand and bowing low instead, kissed it.

It was a very correct kiss, if unexpected. In front of witnesses. On the back of her gloved hand. Of short duration with no excessive lingering. The sort of kiss one would use to say farewell. Completely unremarkable.

Utterly chaste—and yet not at all. Why else had her heart begun to pound? Her knees to quiver? Why should all the hairs on the back of her neck tingle and stand at attention?

"We have an agreement," he said, straightening and raising a brow. "And you may begin by inviting me to escort you to the Westmores' ball tomorrow evening."

"May I ask why?"

"Because her third daughter had a much-whispered about interlude with her brother's French tutor—and Lady X virtually ignored it. I wish to know why. It might lead me to her."

"Oh." She thought a moment. "The Westmores? The house is in Bedford Square is it not?"

"I believe so. Does it matter?"

"It does." She smiled up at him. "Yes. I believe I can make that work."

"Good. Tomorrow, then." He bowed again over her hand —but did not kiss it.

A good thing, she thought, pushing her disappointment away. She wasn't sure her trembling knees could have withstood it.

CHAPTER 4

Chapter Four

*S ociety is thinner right now, with so many gone to enjoy
the festivities of the Hadleigh fair . . .*
  --Whispers from Lady X

A NOVEL SENSATION, actually looking forward to a night at a
ton event. But Tensford couldn't deny his eagerness as he
followed the Earl of Kincade's servant to a formal parlor just
off the entry hall.

"I will inform Lady Hope of your arrival," the footman
said with a bow. He left the parlor door open as he left.

Coming from a family heavy with females, Tensford was
more than passing familiar with the sounds of a household
readying its women to go out. Doors opened and shut above,
feet scurried up stairs and down passages. Whispers and

hurried orders drifted downward—and so did one exchange clearly not meant for him.

"This is the outside of enough!" It sounded like the countess—and her hiss echoed in the two-story hall. "First you insult poor Bardham, and now you entertain the pretensions of such a man! One whose horrid nicknames live in the scandal sheets!"

"Lord Bardham has a nickname, too, did you know?" Lady Hope answered calmly. "*Boredom*, that's was what he was called at school, I have learned." Her tone firmed. "He would be known by quite a different designation, however, if it was more widely known how he treats young ladies. Lord Tensford, on the other hand, has treated me with respect and kindness."

"And why do you think? It's well known that he hasn't two shillings to rub together."

"And once again, Lord Tensford comes out ahead, Catherine. For while everyone whispers that he has no money, I've never heard a hint that he owes a sum to any man. Now move aside, please. The earl is waiting and I've no wish to be late."

Lady Kincade's virulent complaints continued for a moment, but Tensford didn't hear it. He was quite occupied with another novel sensation—a warm buzz of amazement and gratitude. Lady Hope Brightley was *defending* him. Him. Lord Terror. Lord Tender.

It was entirely new. And surprisingly . . . touching. It kindled a small, warm flame in his chest, in the dark, echoing chamber where he usually stored his stoic indifference and stubborn determination.

" . . . and you didn't even have the wits to ask for your brother's escort tonight!" The countess was still complaining. Her voice sounded closer now, though. They must be coming downstairs. "Who knows if a man like that can even afford a carriage to get you there and back?"

He'd heard enough. In a breach of manners he couldn't give a damn about, he stood and strode out into the hall.

And completely forgot his ire for a moment.

Damnation, Lady Hope was lovely. Her gown, dark pink with an embroidered white overlay, made her skin gleam. Against the pale expanse her hair looked like dark, rich silk. She looked expensive and elegant—and entirely too good for him.

But then she spotted him—and her smile lit up the hall like a beacon.

Too good for him? The whisper came from somewhere deep. *The hell with that.*

"Good evening," she called, rounding the last landing. "I apologize if I've kept you waiting."

Behind her, her sister-in-law pursed her lips shut.

"Not at all," he replied. "But we should be going. You'll be pleased to hear, Lady Kincade, that Miss Nichols and her mother are waiting in the carriage outside. Although I can well afford to transport Lady Hope about London, tonight I can save a few shillings. I'll be sure to rub them together in your honor."

The countess's mouth snapped open, then closed again. Lady Hope was trying not to grin as she let the footman help her into her cloak.

Tensford took her arm, nodded to the countess, and strode for the door. Yes, indeed. It was a good start to what he hoped would be a better night.

* * *

THE RECEIVING line at Lady Westmore's snaked, unexpectedly long, through the fine London townhouse. Hope didn't mind. Miss Nichols and her mama, just ahead, were occupied greeting their many friends and acquaintances. She, on the other hand, was quite occupied admiring her escort.

So tall and erect, he stood. Stern. Unmistakably assured. And everyone stared. They tried and tried to knock him down with their whispers, raised brows and sly glances, but he refused to be cowed. It had the opposite effect, in fact. He looked like a sleek cat set amongst the pigeons, too proud to be interested in such, dull, uninspiring prey.

How annoying they must find him.

How alluring *she* found him.

But now was not the time for that. Only a tigress could tame the tiger. She had to be smart and stealthy.

"I'm sorry if you were uncomfortable in the carriage," she told him. "I didn't expect Mrs. Nichols to warn you off her daughter so bluntly."

He shot her a wry grin. "It was unexpected, but actually I found it refreshing. She stated the situation plainly and now we all know where we stand. I think we'll all get along the better for it." Looking ahead, he lowered his voice a little. "I did find it surprising that Miss Nichols has no intention of marrying soon. Is not the firing off of daughters the whole idea of the Season—and quickly, with the least expense?"

Hope glanced fondly at her friend. "Not for that family. She is an only child and her parents quite dote on her. Miss Nichols is quite the favorite this Season and I believe all three of them are having a grand time. It's no wonder they would wish to repeat it next year."

"What of you?" he asked. "I gather your sister-in-law wishes you to marry. This is your first Season, I believe? What do you wish out of it?"

"Catherine wants me out of her house, it's true, but she only wishes me to consider her candidate."

"Bardham," he said with disgust.

"Yes. He's vile—and persistent."

She hadn't thought it possible for him to grow more intense, but he stiffened and every plane on his face sharpened. "He's bothered you again?"

"Not bothered, precisely. But he does seem to pop up everywhere when I am out. The park, the shops, the lending library. Suddenly, I'll look up—and there he is."

"I'll warn him off." His tone had gone tighter, too.

"Thank you, but I don't think it will be necessary. Truly, I believe he's flabbergasted. I'm not sure anyone has ever refused him anything, before."

Tensford frowned. "He never liked to lose, or be denied anything. Only so much fuss a gentleman can make about either, but he did always skirt the boundaries."

She shrugged. "Something will distract him soon enough. In any case, to answer your question—I came to Town just hoping to enjoy myself," she said wistfully.

"Your first Season was delayed—and your parents are gone. I gather those two are related?" he asked with sympathy.

"Yes. Papa died unexpectedly and swiftly." She tried to keep her tone brisk and matter of fact. "Mama's illness began just after we left off mourning—and it lingered."

In the most horrid manner, it had gone on, sapping the strength and everything else from her gentle mother. For so long, Hope's world had consisted of darkened rooms and long nights and endless attempts to tempt her mother's nonexistent appetite or distract her from her ever-present pain. When she had finally emerged from her second mourning, she had wanted only freedom, light, air and laughter. "I want art and music and dancing and to visit all of the sights in London. I want the freedom to breathe and to play and to plan and to think about the ways I can be productive and useful in my life."

"And what of the marriage mart?" he asked, indicating the crowd around them. "Is a husband not part of that future life?"

"Of course," she said a little irritably. "Neither my younger sister nor I will be able to avoid marriage. But I will choose—and not a man like Bardham."

"No," he agreed firmly.

"I've earned that much," she said, feeling righteous and a little belligerent. "And my brother will not sway me. I'll make my own choice, and when I find the right man I will move heaven and earth to get him."

Quite unexpectedly, he stepped closer. He stared down at her with those bright blue eyes and it happened again. The air between them fairly danced, it was so charged. "I believe you will," he rasped.

"Lady Hope? *Ahem.*" Someone cleared a throat.

She started. It was their turn. They'd reached their hosts in the line. Lord and Lady Westmore welcomed her warmly, and though they appeared a little surprised to find Tensford with her, they welcomed him, as well.

They moved quickly through the rest of the family and emerged at the end of the line to find Miss Nichols and her mama waiting. Tensford stood, looking about at the parlors set with dining tables on either side of the passage and the doors ahead of them, standing open to the ballroom.

"What do you think of the Westmore's home?" he asked her.

Surprised at the question, she looked around. "It looks very fine tonight." She frowned at the ice blue wallpaper featured in both parlors and the many glass and china accents. "I wonder if it might not feel . . . cold, perhaps, when it is not filled with guests."

"I wondered the same thing."

"Come along, you two!" Mrs. Nichols called. "Reserve a dance with the ladies while you may, Lord Tensford," she ordered. "I predict these two will be kept very busy tonight."

"Of course." He received the promise of a quadrille with Miss Nichols and then turned to Hope.

"I'll be so bold as to grant you the supper dance, my lord," she said, sparkling up at him. "I confess, I'll be very curious to hear all of your . . . observations of the evening."

"It will be a pleasure." Making his bow, he shot her a grin and moved off into the crowd.

She watched him go, the tiger once more, lithe and fluid, searching amongst the wildebeests for his prey.

"Shoulders back, girls." Mrs. Nichols snapped open her fan. "The gentlemen approach."

* * *

IT WAS TRUE, Tensford had wished nothing more than to strangle a couple of the lordlings who had so mocked him, but he knew the manly importance of being able to take a joke. His forbearance had done him good, it seemed. A few of his contemporaries had approached him to commiserate.

"Young idiots," Lord Montbarrow said with a roll of his eyes. "They'll find some other poor sod to torture, in good time."

It sounded similar to what Lady Hope had said of Bardham. He could see her from their corner of the ballroom. She looked flushed and lovely as she went through the rigorous steps of a country-dance.

"Eh, Tensford?"

He started. "I'm sorry?"

The viscount pursed his lips as he looked Tensford over. "I don't suppose it's true that you locked your aunt away in the attics on bread and water?"

"Worse," Tensford replied, deadpan. "I put an end to her outrageous household expenses." He looked to the heavens. "She was buying new livery to suit every season and when I refused to build her a conservatory, she hired an army of gardeners to keep fires going in the orchard, in an attempt to grow palm trees larger than the ones in her neighbor's hothouse."

"What puts these maggots in their heads?" one of the other gentlemen asked. "My mother keeps ten dogs and two small pageboys to follow the lot of them around all day. The boys carry bones and biscuits for the dogs and extra shawls and quills and gloves for my mother, so that she never has to run and fetch the smallest thing." He shook his head. "I wish I could cut her expenses."

"Oh, I did worse," Tensford confessed. "I closed up the estate house where my aunt was living to save the expense, and forced her to move into the dower house with my mother."

Someone sucked in a breath. "You might as well have stuck her in the attics."

They all laughed.

"Yes. The damned house has twenty rooms, but apparently that's not close to enough for the two of them."

"It wouldn't be enough for me either, had I to live with my mother," Montbarrow said with a shiver.

They compared familial horror stories for a while, then moved on to discuss the latest crop of debutantes.

"A smallish group this year."

"Yes, and more than one who is a bit . . . rambunctious," Montbarrow remarked. "There are a couple who should take care before they end up on the wrong side of Lady X's pen, like poor Tensford, here."

"Yes," someone said, low and snide. "And none more than the youngest of our host."

"Not the young Lady Margaret?" Tensford strove to sound surprised.

"Yes, her. She looks coltish and innocent, but I hear she has a temper—and a defiant streak."

"Lady X may write what she wants of the girl, but it will never get published. Not even if it has more substance than Tensford's supposed sins," Mr. Neville, a younger son of the Baron Longley, said with a raised brow.

"Why not?" Montbarrow asked, indignant on Tensford's behalf.

"Perhaps she is Lady X," Tensford threw out.

"No, it's because Westmore is great friends with the man who prints the paper, Childers. Boyhood chums. His family will never feel the sting of Lady X's sharp wit."

"Chit's too young to be Lady X, in any case," Montbarrow said thoughtfully. "Her scandal rag has been printed for years."

"And people have been trying to ferret her out for just as long." Neville emptied his glass. "We'll never know."

"Perhaps *she* is a *he*," Tensford said, just to keep the conversation going.

"Now there is a thought I hadn't entertained." Montbarrow looked much struck.

"No—couldn't be. She shows far too much interest in fashion," Neville laughed. "And I mean the ribbons and furbelows, not in how easily they might come off!"

The laughter was lower and more conspiratorial this time

—as was the conversation that followed, about much different sorts of women.

Tensford didn't listen. Disappointment tasted bitter in the back of his throat. But this was just his first attempt. He sighed. There would be other ideas—perhaps a visit to the printer might turn something up—and this night held promise to be the first he might actually enjoy in London. He'd gained a modicum of acceptance from his peers—and he still had his dance with Lady Hope to look forward to.

He watched her throughout the evening, so clearly enjoying herself, just as she'd wished, and he realized her mere presence made him feel more at ease. And that it made him happy to see her happy. But it also made him . . . impatient.

The more time he spent with her, the more he was drawn to her. He liked her smile. He liked the way she could listen with sympathy and not pity. Hell, he liked the way she actually listened, truly hearing what he said, without merely waiting for her turn to speak, to lecture, or to ask for things he couldn't give.

He liked the way her hair shone in the candlelight and how she looked both curvy and elegant in that dress.

Two thousand pounds.

A handsome sum, but it lost in the balance against the sheer number of leaking roofs and crumbling barns at Greystone, not to mention the tenants in need of steady work.

So he curbed his impatience. He talked with the gentlemen and even danced twice. And he squashed the eagerness and anticipation he felt when the time came for the supper dance and he could approach her at last. He kept his smile relaxed and he kept a rein on the tightening in his nether regions—all in spite of the way her low bodice hugged her curves and the rich color of her gown enhanced the flush of her skin.

He bowed before her. "I believe this is our dance."

His hand held steady, his manner elegantly detached.

He convinced himself that he could do this.

And then the first strains of the music began.

A waltz.

A cursed waltz, where he was going to have to touch her, hold her, feel her hands on him.

Damn.

CHAPTER 5

Have we, as a Society, given thanks for the waltz? Oh, but we must. To feel your partner move beneath your touch, to feel his arms around you . . . surely it is the most romantic dance of all time . . .

--Whispers From Lady X

HER HEART POUNDED when the supper dance arrived—at last. Her excitement was partially due to her daring plan, of course, but that was not the full of it.

Why did it feel like *relief* when Lord Tensford approached? Gladness and relief, as if it had been a trial to spend the evening away from his side?

Breathing deeply, she managed to stay calm when he bowed over her hand—an effort that grew easier when the music sounded the first few strains of a waltz—and he looked horrified.

She laughed. "Do relax, my lord. I promise not to step on your toes."

The stoic mask dropped back into place. "I wish I could promise the same, but it's been some time since I waltzed."

"You are safe with me. Should you miss a step, I vow not to show a sign of it."

His mouth quirked. "Very well." He held out a hand. "Let's muddle through, shall we?"

He led her out and eased them into the dance. The music swelled. Their eyes met—and the world went blurry at the edges. No need for her to dissemble, despite his worries. Effortlessly they moved together while the dancers, musicians, and all the rest of the ball disappeared in a colorful haze, melted by the heat of his hand at her waist. She shivered suddenly, as the warmth began to spread, chasing cold and doubt and fear away.

Time slowed. She drifted, weightless, in his arms. Even the music had faded inside the bubble they'd slipped into. A place where they were connected in a way she had never imagined.

Yes. This, whispered her soul. And she knew her instincts had been right and this was exactly where they were meant to be.

Except it wasn't.

Not yet.

So she blinked and the world came back into focus and he, too, looked like he was awakening from a dream.

Gradually, her wits returned. "So, how did you fare in your hunt, my lord?"

"I . . . hunt?" He sounded more than a little befuddled.

"For Lady X?" she prompted.

"Oh." He shook his head a little. "I hit a bit of a wall."

"I hope you won't be offended if I say I am glad."

His gaze cleared as he met hers directly. "You don't think she deserves to be held up to the same scrutiny that she focuses on others?"

"I think revenge or retaliation rarely does anyone good, and can rebound upon the person seeking it."

A thunderous frown wrinkled his brow and he fell silent for a moment. "Perhaps I don't need to expose her. But I do wish to confront her. I want her to look at me and hear about the shambles she's contributed to in my life."

Hope didn't respond. The waltz was coming to an end. She squeezed Tensford's hand. "My lord, I've fulfilled my end of the bargain, bringing you tonight. Now it is your turn. The dance is winding down. Can you make sure we end it near those potted plants?" She nodded toward the corner.

Surprise, and a mix of mischief and curiosity, chased his frown away. He nodded. "I am a man of my word, Lady Hope."

The waltz ended. The musicians stood and stretched and set their instruments aside. Couples joined the guests moving toward the rooms set up for dining, but Hope pushed Tensford behind the palms, placed conveniently to hide a servant's door.

"All of the servants are occupied with dinner," she whispered. "The way should be clear."

She slipped through the door and started down a narrow set of stairs.

He followed. "What are you up to? Have you an heiress hidden down in a coal larder?"

"No. Shhh!" The stairs let out onto a wide passage. Kitchen sounds and barked orders sounded at the far end. She peered out, watching for her moment. "Now!"

She dashed a short distance toward a wide door. He followed and then they were through, and out in the night air.

"Quickly," she told him. "We have to get there and back before the late supper is finished."

She pulled him past stacked crates, a privy and the

kitchen gardens. A gate in the back led to a narrow street that stood between the house grounds and the mews.

"What are you doing, Lady Hope?" he whispered, balking at last. "You cannot wander in the mews and back lanes! It could be dangerous."

She shook her head. "Bedford Square, my lord, if you will recall? It's all locked up tight." She gestured behind them, where the lane narrowed and eventually ended at a locked gate. "Perfectly safe."

"Unless you don't get back before you are missed!"

"Miss Nichols will cover for us. There are two separate dining areas. She'll just tell her mama she saw us in the other one."

He considered that. "But where in blazes are you taking us?"

"Just up here." She dragged him along the row of houses. At the fourth one she stopped and traversed a path to the house that echoed the one they had already taken, where she knocked on the closed door.

It opened immediately. "Come in quickly, Miss." The maid led them further into the house and to a staircase on the other side of the similarly wide passage. The house lay dark and mostly quiet around them, although the clink of dishes could be heard from the kitchen area ahead. "This one leads to the family wing. Stop at the third landing and you'll know where you are."

"Thank you, Mary. We won't be long." She started up the stairs.

Lord Tensford did not immediately follow.

"Hurry on, sir," Mary urged. "It's best for everyone if you are not seen."

Hope breathed a sigh of relief as his footsteps started after her.

"Whose house is this?" he whispered. "What in hell's bells are you up to, young lady?"

She didn't answer, just exited the stairway and counted doors until she found the right one, opened it and entered.

He stopped on the threshold.

She beckoned him in.

"I think I will require an explanation before I enter a young lady's bedroom," he said sardonically.

She crossed her arms. "I took a gamble bringing you here, Tensford. I did it because I know you are not Lord Terror, no matter what the *ton* says. I trust you. Now it is for you to decide. Do you trust me?"

Heaving an exasperated sigh, he stepped in. "If we are caught . . ."

"We will not be caught." She closed the door behind him and turned up the two small lamps in the room. "This is the home of my friend, Miss Emma Atherton."

"If you wished me to meet her—"

"That's not why I brought you here," she interrupted. "Miss Atherton is a fine young lady, but she and her family are away from Town, attending the Hadleigh fair." She turned to him and put her hands on her hips. "I said I would prove to you that worthy young ladies do exist in the peerage. Miss Atherton is one, and she allowed me to set this up, so I could tell you about another. I want you to judge this girl's heart, without the bias of family, connections, or money to interfere."

"Anonymously," he said.

"Yes." Eagerly she gestured toward a writing desk. It was cluttered with fashion magazines, sketches, notes and letters. "I wanted to show you these. They belong to a young lady who was brought to London with her family, all save for a younger sister left at home. The younger girl is lame, you see. A withered leg, I believe. The light, diaphanous fashions of the last years put her at a disadvantage, emphasizing her uneven gait and crooked stance. It has made the girl shy about meeting people or appearing in public."

"A shame." He frowned. "She would do better to let it show without comment. If she treats it as matter-of-fact, others will too, eventually. Though it may take some time." He shrugged. "In any case, there's no use hiding."

Was that what he was attempting, with the state of his own misfortunes? She'd seen the gentlemen talking with him earlier. Perhaps he was right, and it would work for him.

"Her sister certainly wishes for the girl to go out into the world more. The fashions are changing, you see. Waists are lowering, fabrics are growing more varied, and heavier. This girl is searching out fabrics at linen drapers and in the shops of all the modistes. She's making notes of fashions and how they might be adjusted. She's drawing pictures and giving elaborate descriptions about current fashions and the ladies who wear them and the events to which they are worn. It's a letter campaign, full of excitement and ideas. She's trying to convince her sister that new styles and heavier fabrics will help disguise the first, obvious notice of her condition, working to persuade her that a slow and careful gait can look elegant and not just different."

He was listening. She could see it. But he hadn't yet taken the point.

She moved to pick up a letter. "I wanted you to see that this young lady is more than a flirt and a careless gossip. She might have frivolous moments. I'm sure we all do. But she's investing a substantial amount of time into this project and in trying to draw her sister into the idea, developing her interest, and coaxing her out of her nest."

He nodded. "It is admirable. I grant you that." He gazed across the cluttered desk. "It's a lot of work and a fine cause. I wish her success."

She relaxed. She hadn't been sure he would see what she wanted to show him.

He gave her a pointed look. "You have a younger sister at home, do you not?"

There it was. She'd been worried that he eventually would begin to put pieces together and make connections—and it was the first thing out of his mouth.

"Yes." She allowed herself to smile at the thought of her hey-go-mad sister. "Her name is Glory. Oh, and she's a handful, that one. My brother is going to have a time taming her and I look forward to watching from afar." She laughed. "Although, if he is smart he will just bribe her with a prime, blooded mare. Glory is horse mad. She's probably riding hell-for-leather across the Downs even as we speak."

She dropped herself into the desk chair. "But you have a sister as well." She waved a hand over the collection of papers. "I'm sure you understand the urge to help out a sibling."

He shrugged. "My sister is older than I. The relationship is different."

"Are you two not . . . amicable?" The thought troubled her.

"We were friends once, when we were younger. Though she swears I was a terrible pest, she did relent to my pleading once in a while and consent to a game of spillikins or hoops. She also hosted elaborate tea parties for her dolls and learned that our cook would provide real cakes if she invited me." He chuckled.

"What happened?"

"We grew older. I was sent to school. She married and became concerned only with her status amongst the ladies of the *ton*." His mouth twisted. "I think that now she could give your sister-in-law a run for Most Shrill."

Hope shivered.

"Yes. But it's not all bad. She's not thrilled with me at the moment because I don't have the funds to fulfill her latest loan request, but as she's married and gone, she's not utterly furious with me for destroying her status in the neighborhood at home."

"Oh. Your mother?"

"And my aunt as well," he nodded.

"Because of the rumors?"

"No. Because I leased Greystone Park."

She frowned, trying to understand.

"Not the entire estate. Not the dower house where my mother and aunt live. Not the farms or orchards or tenancies. Just the main house and the gardens. I leased them to a merchant named McNamara. He's obtained a staggering amount of success with his shipping concerns. He has the money, and now he wants his wife and daughter to learn the ways of the gentry so that he might get a noble grandson. He decided to give them a trial run in country society before he launches them on London."

Silently, she absorbed all this. Then she frowned. "But then where do you live?" He hadn't said *we* when he mentioned the dower house.

"I took one of the empty tenant's cottages."

She blinked.

"It's just temporary. The lease was only for a year. Not far to go on it now. My mother despised the idea—and she only grew angrier when she met Mrs. McNamara. But it had to be done. There were urgent needs on the estate and no money for this year's seed, had I not done something."

"You amaze me, Tensford."

He laughed. "When my mother says that, she doesn't mean it as a compliment."

"I do." She shook her head. "I greatly admire your ingenuity, not to mention your resilience and your commitment to your people."

"Yes, well, my people are well worth it." He picked up a rough sketch from the desk. "My own family may not be . . . close, but there are any number of devoted families at Greystone. And you speak of sibling connections? One of my tenants has a pair of twin boys. You've never seen such a bond. I swear, they can hatch a plot with just a shared look. No conversation required."

She laughed.

He took her hand and pulled her from the chair. "I want you to know I understand what you meant to show me here. It is good to know that there are such family attachments in Society, too."

She heaved a sigh. It had been a gamble, but he had responded just as she'd hoped.

"But truly, we must get back." He grimaced. "I don't want to give Lady X a real scandal to write about."

"Yes, let's go. The dancing will begin again soon, no doubt."

Silently, they slipped back the way they had come, moving together like shadows through the darkened house and along the quiet lane. As he held open the Westmore's gate, though, he leaned in. "You do know, Lady Hope, that you are fortunate that I enjoy your company?"

She paused.

He eased the gate closed. "This is the second ball I've spent in your company and gone unfed."

She laughed softly. "Oh! I hadn't considered . . . I am sorry, my lord."

"It's fine," he said airily. "Unless I hear there were lobster patties—and then I will have to seriously reconsider our friendship."

"Then I will pray that Lady Westmore served only cold,

uninspired sandwiches." She cracked the door leading to the servant's hall and peered in. "All clear!" She ducked in and raced for the back stairway, feeling him hot on her heels. She rushed upward. "Oh, I hear the musicians tuning their instruments!" she threw over her shoulder. Picking up her skirts, she climbed faster.

He caught her at the top, taking hold of her arm before she could test the door leading into the ballroom.

"Hold a moment. I confess, I am enjoying your scheming, Lady Hope. I can't wait to see what you'll come up with next. But we've successfully evaded exposure so far, this evening. I'd hate for a stray curl to betray us at the end." His eyes smiling, he caught a lock of hair that she'd hadn't felt slip its moors.

The smile faded, though, as he tucked it back into place, adjusting a hairpin to anchor it. His gaze grew heated as, almost reverently, he leaned in to press his face into her coiffure. He breathed deeply. "Rosemary," he said roughly.

Her pulse still raced from the climb. She felt hot and flushed and a tad out of breath—and happy. More than that. Triumphant. His hand lingered in her hair. Without thought, she leaned toward him. They breathed together, sharing the same air, feeling the same . . . want.

His hand slid down, trailing along the curve of her neck, sending shivers up and down her spine, and then, easily, naturally, she stood on her toes and kissed him.

He stiffened.

A great shudder passed through him. She thought he would rear back, but instead he yanked her closer. She had started it, but he quickly took over, moving his mouth over hers, searching for and finding all the ways their lips fit together.

Desire was a spear that passed through and held her fast.

Everything else was lost in heat and the forbidden thrill of his lips coaxing hers and the velvet touch of his tongue.

His hands moved to her back. She tilted her head as the kiss deepened, but then gasped in shock and pleasure as he brought her hard against him and she was confronted with the large and thrilling evidence of his enthusiasm.

The sound must have broken the spell. He ended the kiss, dragging his hands from her and taking a step back.

She stared up at him, breathing heavily.

Silence stretched between them.

"Bad idea," he whispered.

"But—"

"No. We cannot." He said it flatly.

On the other side of the wall, a sprightly reel struck up.

"You should go out there." He gestured.

"Alone?"

"Yes. If someone asks, say you needed a maid to help you with your gown."

"You'll follow?"

He waved her on.

She stepped to the door, looked back over her shoulder. "I would offer an apology, but it would be a lie."

Without waiting for an answer, she slipped into the ballroom and strolled casually out from behind the palms. She quickly found an acquaintance nearby and struck up a conversation.

He did not follow. And once more, she watched and waited for him to appear.

He never emerged.

CHAPTER 6

Dynastic marriages, political alliances, unification of lands or fortunes, love matches. There are many reasons for marriage in Society, my dear young ladies. Be sure that the one you end up with works for you . . .

--Whispers from Lady X

TENSFORD WOKE the next morning after a bad night, and still in a dark mood.

Foolish. Foolish. Foolish. What an idiot he'd been, to kiss Lady Hope Brightley.

He'd made sacrifices, attempting to restore Greystone. Most had barely registered. He didn't miss his rooms at the manor house—they had been a refuge from his mother's harangues, but not more. He couldn't care less about eating simply or bemoan spending his time working out on the estate, next to his people.

But he'd felt a twinge at selling his sporty curricle and he'd hated passing up fossil hunting jaunts with Sterne.

That kiss, however, was another thing entirely. He'd walked right up to the edge of a precipice with that one.

She was so damned tempting. Soft and full of wit and humor—and passion. She'd gone to so much trouble, put her own reputation at risk, just to soothe his troubled spirit and make him more at ease with . . . the world. And to perhaps find a girl who would see past his money troubles and into his heart?

It was a kind gesture, generous and . . . dangerous.

He didn't want another girl—he wanted more of her. And he didn't want to want her.

He didn't want to find himself having to sacrifice her.

Still fuming at the imbalances of fate, he went down to the breakfast room . . . and stopped dead on the threshold.

His mother sat at the table.

"There you are, Tensford. Don't stand there gaping like a fish. Do come in. Breakfast is waiting."

He gaped at the groaning sideboard. "So I see. What is this, Mother? Why are you here?"

"I have come for the Season. It's time I had a bit of a frolic." She made a face. "Your aunt has worn my nerves to a frazzle—and that McNamara woman! Between the two of them I thought I might go mad. So, here I am."

To drive him mad? He went to stare at the array of food. "Are we expecting guests? At breakfast?"

"That is a typical breakfast for an English lord, Tensford. Hundreds of peers across London are surveying the same sort of spread. You are an earl. It's time you lived like one."

"I am an earl with few funds. We are a family with very little money, Mother." Thanks in largest part to her. "And I've told you time and again, you must learn to live like it."

"You don't mean that I should scrape and pinch in London, surely?" she asked, aghast.

"I do. Unless you wish me to have to lease this house, as well?"

Horror filled her expression. "You wouldn't!"

"I would. We eat simply here, Mother. We live simply. If you cannot abide by this one necessary edict, you may take yourself off to a hotel for the Season. I know your widow's portion will cover the expense."

He had never asked her to contribute her funds to aid Greystone's failing conditions.

She had never offered.

She waved off his suggestion, now. "That money must go to the modistes. It's been several years since I came to Town. I am in need of a new wardrobe if I am to assist as chaperone to Miss McNamara."

He set his plate down, still empty. "Miss McNamara?"

"Yes. Although the mother is a forward, vulgar thing, the daughter is quite easy to get along with."

Quite willing to stroke his mother's vanity, he suspected.

"The girl has been everything friendly and is very eager to learn. When she was invited to stay with friends in London this spring, she begged me to come along and show her how to get on."

And to gain her entrance into Society events, no doubt.

"I daresay she will become quite a success. Really, Tensford, you should look to her before she is snatched out from under your nose."

Before he could reply to this sally, Higgins appeared in the doorway. "Miss McNamara has arrived, sir."

He looked to his mother.

She looked away. "Oh, I did invite her to breakfast with us, as she and I are going to start our shopping this morning."

"Good morning!" Miss McNamara breezed into the room, going straight to his mother and stopping to kiss her on the cheek. "My dear Lady Tensford." She stood and smiled at him, then dropped into a credible curtsy. "Lord Tensford. Thank you for the kind invitation."

He nodded. She was pretty, in a sharp corners and angular planes sort of way. He'd met her several times before and found her swift, darting gaze to be unnerving. Mostly because he sensed a cold and calculating mind behind it.

"Come and sit beside me, Miss McNamara. Tensford will fill you a plate."

"Oh, thank you. How lovely." Seating herself, she looked around with interest. "Your home is quite remarkable, my lord. Portman Square is so very impressive." She raised her brows toward his mother. "And quite fashionable, is it not?"

"Of course," his mother assured her.

The women spoke a little of the best London addresses and then moved on to the best London shops. Tensford fixed a plate for their guest and one for himself.

His mother rose just as he moved to sit and eat.

"I've finished," she announced. "I'll just go and fetch my things before we go. You two talk a little, get to know each other. I'll only be a moment."

He stared after her. He'd never seen her fetch anything in his life, not for herself or anyone else.

Silence reigned for a few moments, broken only by the clink of silver on china.

"Your mother is very kind," Miss McNamara said eventually.

He made a noncommittal sound and covered it with a bite of bacon.

"I suppose you know she thinks to push us together."

He looked up to find her watching him with a measuring eye.

"I hadn't thought to go along with it at first." Her gaze roamed over him. "Too provincial, I thought. But you do look a sight better in your Town clothes, my lord." She pointed with her fork. "I prefer this version over the dusty farmer."

His jaw tightened.

"Then, too, I did not understand how marriages work amongst the peerage, but now I do."

"Then you have me at a disadvantage. I do not know what you mean."

She leaned forward. "Let us not talk around it. You have the title and the land. I have the money." Her shoulder lifted. "I doubt I'll have trouble providing you the requisite heir and spare, and once they are safely ensconced in the nursery . . . we can each do what we wish."

"What we wish?" he croaked, astonished.

"Yes. You enjoy the country life, down to the lowest aspects. I've seen you at work on the barns or in the fields." She shuddered. "I find it all exceedingly dull. I prefer the excitement of Town. You can stay on the estate and perhaps I will take this place." She looked around, nodding. "I could do quite a bit with it, given time and money." She smiled at him. "You'll have your life. I'll have mine. *Et voilà!* Everyone is happy."

He sat, stunned, while an image rose, of such a future. It was all too easy to imagine, unfortunately. Yet his brain shied away.

Instead it tried to conjure a different picture. One with a smiling Lady Hope seated across from him. Easy laughter, teasing. Heat and kisses. He wondered if she liked the country—

No. He stood, cutting off that line of thinking.

Damnation.

"Enjoy your shopping, Miss McNamara."

She sat back, watching him with a brow raised.

"Please tell my mother that I had an urgent matter to attend to. Good day."

He left the house, stamping anger, panic and frustration into the pavement. This, this at last seemed too much to ask of him.

For a long time, he wandered. It rained a bit. People pushed past him, eager to get in out of the weather. He couldn't think. His mind had gone numb. When he bothered to look up, he found himself on Fleet Street.

An idea bloomed.

Lady X. Her gossipy tidbits were current—and they were printed daily. And here was the largest gathering of printers in London. Surely the lady would not deliver her pieces to the printer herself, but she must have a regular system set up.

He could find her. He could. He longed to confront her and he needed something to occupy his mind beyond his intolerable situation—and he needed an excuse to be from home.

What had that name been? The printer who was friendly with Lord Westmore?

Childers.

He set out, reading all the signs of the printers, pubs, booksellers and mapmakers along the way. He found them, at last, in Ludgate Hill. *Childers & Son, Lithographers, Printers & Engravers.*

Standing outside the shop, he considered the matter. A clerk pushed by him to enter. He couldn't follow every person who made a delivery to the place, but it was a daily sheet. There would be a pattern. He just needed to discover it. Looking around, he spotted a coffee shop across the way, several doors down.

Perfect.

Watching the traffic, he set out for the place, his resolve firming as he went.

* * *

THREE DAYS LATER, Tensford was still seated in the coffee house. He'd barely been home, returning only to sleep, to fetch paper, ink and quills, and to sort through his mail.

He'd made friends with Mrs. Fitz, the gregarious, comfortable lady who ran the coffee house. He'd become somewhat addicted to her special spiced *café au lait*, rich with Eastern flavor. He'd shared with her Mrs. Agnew's recipe for scones. And he'd kept copious notes on the comings and goings at *Childers & Son.*

It was a slow period at the moment, so he'd also started making a list.

QUEEN ANNE CHIFFEROBE
 Sevres Ormolu vase
 Silver chafing dish = 2

THE BELL over the door rang. He didn't look up until a shadow fell over the paper in front of him.

"Sterne!" He blinked up at his friend. "How are you?"

"Exasperated. I've been looking for you for days."

"I received your notes. That's why I sent a message to let you know I am fine."

"Yes, and I had to bribe the boy who delivered it to tell me where you sent it from."

Tensford straightened. "That worked, did it?"

"Obviously. Here I am."

He frowned, thinking.

"Tensford?"

"Yes? Oh, sorry. I have considered that route, but it stands to reason she's thought of that already and taken measures against it."

"What are you going on about, man?" Sterne looked around. "Why are you hiding here? Who is *she*?"

"Not hiding. Spying." He explained his mission. "And I've narrowed it down to two likely messengers," he said with excitement. "I'm favoring the three o'clock boy over the early morning lad. It gives her time to decide what to write and to make it . . . jaunty. Would you say that's an accurate description of her style?"

Sterne frowned. "Good God, you're really going to expose Lady X?" He gazed over at the printer's shop. "I'm not sure that's a good idea. The whole thing could turn against you."

"That's what Lady Hope said," Tensford muttered.

"Yes, and she's another who has been wondering where you've disappeared to. She asked me to give you a message, should I see you."

"Well?"

"She hopes you'll be available to drive her in Hyde Park tomorrow."

Tensford heaved a sigh. "It wouldn't be wise." He should avoid the temptation. But he had given her his word.

"Why not?" Sterne asked.

He ignored the question and pulled his list closer. "I'm glad you are here, Sterne. I need to ask a favor of you."

His friend waited expectantly.

"Will you ask your uncle if he might be interested in my sea urchin fossil? The one I keep on my desk? It is an unusual piece. No one else has one like it, that I've seen."

"I know the one. Of course, I will ask. He will likely be interested, but Tensford—I know that fossil is special to you. Your father—" He stopped. "I know what it means. Why would you wish to sell it? Are things so bad?"

"Bad enough, though likely not in the way you are think-ing." He told Sterne about his mother and her candidate for his marriage.

"She sounds cold."

"That's an understatement. And my mother is as bad. She left a note on top of the stack of my mail. It said one thing. Forty thousand pounds."

Sterne dropped into the seat across from him. "Forty thousand . . . hell and damnation."

"Yes. It gets worse. The pair of them lay in wait for me last night, ostensibly enjoying a late cordial and discussing their night at the theatre. The outrageous McNamara chit took me aside and told me that she'd heard the rumors about me and didn't care a snap for them."

"Well, that's promising."

He shuddered. "She said I could be Lord Terror with her, if I so wished, as long as no marks showed afterwards. Or we could find a girl to keep somewhere, as long as, as my wife, she was compensated for her willingness to indulge me."

"Good God," Sterne said, horrified. "You cannot marry her."

"Thus the favor. I'm making a list of everything of value that is not entailed. Perhaps I can put together enough money for that mill idea I told you about."

Sterne still looked stricken. "I know you didn't wish to destroy that old forest."

"I still don't. But neither do I wish to marry this merce-nary in skirts—and no one else is lining up to have me."

"I am sorry."

"I'll replant as I cut," Tensford said, desperate. "It won't be forever." He slumped in his seat. "Just for two hundred years or so."

Sterne sat quietly for a moment. "Listen, Tensford. I think

you need a fresh perspective on your situation. You know I'm staying with my uncle while I'm in Town?"

Tensford frowned. "No. Is your father not in London? What with all the debate over the Corn Laws, I would have thought he'd be in the thick of it."

"He's here," Sterne said flatly. "But as I still have no burning interest in politics, he cannot find any interest at all in me." He rolled his eyes. "It's more comfortable for all of us if I stay with my aunt and uncle." He grinned. "Especially me. And I think you should come over and enjoy an evening with us. How about tomorrow evening?"

He looked over toward the printer's shop. "Yes. Thank you, it sounds—"

He jumped up. "There's the messenger. I'll be there. Tell Lady Hope that I'll take her driving, first. And tell Mrs. Fitz that I'll be back for my things." He bolted for the door, but paused before going through. "Sterne?"

"Yes?"

"Can I borrow your curricle tomorrow?"

His friend laughed. "Yes. And my matched bays as well."

"Thank you!" Tensford darted across the street, narrowly missed a collision with a speeding hack, and slowed his pace when he neared the printer's shop.

The messenger boy left the place, whistling.

Tensford passed him by, ducked into a doorway, then started after the boy, several paces behind.

They traveled back to Fleet Street, heading toward the Strand and the West End. The boy was in no hurry, with his mission accomplished. He greeted several people, stopped to speak with a street sweeper and bought a sweet bun from a woman with a cart.

It wasn't until he'd stuffed in the last of the bun that something set him on alert, or his instincts kicked in. He started to walk faster. At a corner he stopped, looking back and taking note of everyone behind him.

Acting unconcerned and oblivious, Tensford passed him by. But some stray memory of the same sort of moment earlier must have registered. The boy bolted.

Tensford gave chase. He kept up while the boy stuck to the main street, but when he ducked down one alley and then another, Tensford began to lose ground. The urchin knew the back ways, and obviously where all the bolt-holes and short cuts lay. Tensford lost him.

Damnation.

He gave up, finally, and began the long walk back to Ludgate.

CHAPTER 7

*W**here is our Lord Tender? The gentleman has scarcely been seen in Society for days. Rumor has it that certain other members of his family have arrived in Town, perhaps that is the reason?*

--Whispers from Lady X

THE NEXT DAY the sun shone down on a fine, spring day in Mayfair. Sterne had his rig all ready to go when Tensford arrived.

He let out a long, low whistle. "I'll say it again, these bays are beauties. Sure you want to loan them to me?"

"I've seen you drive to an inch. The bays will be fine. But dare I trust you to the hands of Lady Hope? She seems a resourceful girl."

"She's quite a wonderful girl," he corrected.

When Sterne waited expectantly, he sighed. "With a dowry of two thousand."

"Ah. I thought you seemed as if you were in something of a quandary."

Tensford didn't respond.

Sterne stopped him before he climbed aboard the curricle. "You recall, you've promised to return for dinner? My aunt and uncle have got together a little party, and they are expecting you."

"I'll be here. Thank you for keeping my kit upstairs for me. And thank you, Sterne, for allowing me to take your rig out just a bit early."

His friend looked troubled, but he nodded. "I'll see you tonight."

It took a while to get through the busy streets. Everyone was out enjoying the sunshine today, it seemed. But he pulled up before *Childers & Son* near the proper time.

Only a few moments passed before the boy appeared. He was early. He moved quickly and watched the faces on the pavement as he approached. He hadn't yet looked to the parked rig.

Tensford waited until the lad nearly reached the door. He gave a short whistle and an order. "Do not run."

The boy froze. He looked over and up—and his eyes widened when he saw the gold sovereign that Tensford held aloft.

"Tell your employer that I wish to talk. I have questions to ask and things to say to her, but I wish her no harm."

Eyes still on the coin, the boy nodded. Tensford tossed it to him, took up the reins, and pulled away.

* * *

HOPE WATCHED AT THE WINDOW, praying he would come. She hadn't seen Tensford in days. She was gambling and she knew it. She just hoped she hadn't already lost the game.

She gave a little hop of joy when he pulled up before the house. She ran straight from the room, hoping to meet him before her sister-in-law could say anything scathing to him.

She paused on the landing, however, when Catherine came forward from the back of the house. Her brother James and Lord Bardham were with her.

Hope suppressed a groan.

"There are maps in here," Catherine said, going into the study. "But the area is huge. How could anyone know—"

Her words faded as she went further. Her brother followed her. But Bardham looked upward before he entered —and caught sight of her on the stairs. Closing the door, he stood and waited.

Sighing, she continued down.

"Lady Hope."

"Lord Bardham." Her maid trailed down the stairs after her, bringing her bonnet and gloves. Hope took them. "If you'll excuse me, I'm going out."

He stepped closer and the maid fled.

"I am willing to overlook the insult you paid me at the Loxtons'." His breath smelled sour. "Why don't we start over again?"

She raised her chin. "Because I will not forgive your ungentlemanly behavior that night, nor the harm you meant to do me."

"So fine you find the moral high ground, my lady." He reached out and grabbed her wrist. "I know your secret. I have need of that money."

"Oh, I've a good idea of your secret too, sir." She narrowed her eyes at him. "Two of the partners in your father's canal venture are known swindlers." She nodded toward the study. "Why maps? Looking for details to use to cheat people of their money? Or are you looking for a place to hide after the scheme fails and everyone loses their investment? Everyone but you, that is?"

The purple hue of fury swept over his already reddened features. His grip tightened.

A knock sounded on the door. A footman emerged to answer it.

She snatched her hand away. Lord Tensford stepped into the hall.

"Him? You're going out with *him*?" Bardham ground his teeth. "Why?"

She raked him with a scornful look. "Because he is a gentleman. And you, sir, are not."

"Good afternoon, Lord Tensford," she called, moving toward him.

"Good afternoon, Lady Hope." He bowed. Rising, he fixed Bardham with a warning look, then turned to her without acknowledging him. "Thank you for agreeing to take a drive with me," he said wryly.

She laughed and pulled on her gloves. "Thank *you*, my lord. Shall we go?"

She went out on his arm without looking back.

"Oh, my," she said, as they stepped out. "What a dashing rig."

He grinned. "My wallet may be thin, but I am rich in my friends. Sterne lent me his curricle."

He helped her up. "You are indeed wealthy in your friends," she said as he climbed in and took the reins up with skill. "But only because you are rich in character, sir." She stiffened her spine as they eased out into traffic. "Before we reach the park, I wish to say something."

His mouth twisted. "My hands are full. I doubt I could stop you."

"I want you to know I think you a fine gentleman and I enjoy your friendship. It pains me to see you worry. I think you deserve everything good." She paused. "I offer my apology for the . . . incident at the end of our last adventure. I have no wish to make you uncomfortable in my company."

His gaze slid sideways. "That was a very fine speech."

"I meant it."

"It was a fine kiss, too. I greatly enjoyed it."

"As did I."

"Too much," he said with a sigh, then a great frown. "I don't wish for either of us to be hurt."

"No. Nor do I."

"It's between us . . . the potential, for hurt."

"Yes." He meant heartbreak. But there was also potential for so much more. She was gambling on the *more*.

"Then let us remain friends."

"Friends," she agreed. *For now.* "As a friend, can I ask you to accompany me to tea after the park? I have someplace special in mind." She tossed him an arch look. "It's the next step in my campaign."

"I should be glad to. If you still mean to find a young lady who would have me, I will tell you, I am in need of alternatives."

She'd heard his mother had brought a young lady to Town with her. "I think I can provide you with at least one palatable choice." She crossed her fingers under a fold of her skirt.

He sighed. "It's find an acceptable girl or learn all I can about timber and milling, for I have no taste for my mother's plans."

"Milling?" she asked.

He explained about his idea, and his reluctance to destroy Greystone's old forests.

She shook her head, impressed. "You do not flinch from

hard choices, Lord Tensford. I admire how you handle your difficulties with grace and ingenuity."

He shrugged. "It's only necessity—and while you have not shared all of the facts about your parents and your mother's illness, still, I think you must not be a stranger to stepping in and doing what must be done."

She flushed a little. It was both uncomfortable and strangely wonderful to be seen. To know that someone had looked past her light comments and noticed the painful truth behind them.

They spoke of other things, then, but not in depth, for they'd reached Hyde Park, where the entire fashionable world appeared to be out on the strut. Time and again, they were stopped for a greeting, a compliment or an invitation.

"You seem to be well on your way to being accepted back into the *ton*, my lord."

"Yes, well, the curiosity seekers are due to Lady X. But the cautiously friendly folk are due to you." He was not wearing his stark and impassive look now. In fact, his gaze looked soft and . . . hot. "Thank you."

Her face had grown warm, too. The heat was spreading, from the back of her neck, along her arms . . . and heading south to pool in her belly.

"Shall we leave them behind and go to take our tea?"

Her heart started to hammer. "Yes. Please."

She directed him to Jermyn Street and a bakery called *Le Cygne*. He wondered what she was up to as he paid a lingering boy to watch the bays. They went inside and sat by the window, where the French *Madame* who owned the place took their order herself.

The tea was of good quality and the pastries delectable. He ordered gingerbread and sighed in happiness at the first bite.

"A favorite?" she asked.

"Oh, yes. Cook always made ginger biscuits in the winter months. I would come in from the cold and follow my nose down to the kitchens. I could stay, if there were ginger biscuits. She'd fix me a plate and a tumbler of cold milk. It was always so warm and cheerful down there."

Unlike the rest of the house.

"Our cook's specialty was a currant cake. It was always a grand day when she made them. The smell would drift up and everyone would smile, from my father on down to the chamber maid."

They enjoyed in silence for a moment.

"What do you eat in your tenant cottage?" she asked, eventually.

He shrugged. "Toasted bread and cheese. Fruit from the orchards. Fish from the river." He grinned. "Sometimes I am invited to a tenant's or laborer's home for dinner. Just like those old tea parties with my sister, the cook at Greystone always gives me a game pie or a pot of stew to take with me."

"I'll bet you get a lot of invitations, then," she said with a laugh.

"More than in Town, for sure."

He took another bite, savoring it. "It is a good way to stay connected with my people, keep track of their conditions, and be sure that they are fed well, at least for a day."

Her expression turned solemn. "We are fortunate, all of us who know the comfort of good smells, a warm welcome and a full belly."

"Very true." The bloke who married her would know such comforts, and countless more. He wondered who the damned lucky sod would be.

He hated him already.

"Why was Bardham at your home?" he asked suddenly.

"He's thick with Catherine and her brother. I cannot avoid him entirely."

"If he bothers you, tell me immediately, and I'll—" He'd beat the sodding arse to within an inch of his life. And he'd enjoy every minute of it.

"I think Lord Bardham understands the situation."

"I hope you are right."

Madame Hobert came to their table. "Everything is fine, yes?" She was middle aged, very French and still pretty.

"More than fine. Every bite was delicious." Tensford reached for his purse.

"*Non, non*! Lady Hope and her friends are always welcome, and they do not pay here." She waved him off with a smile.

He looked between the two of them, sure there was a story there.

Lady Hope merely raised her brows at the proprietress.

"Yes, yes." Madame Hobert nodded toward the back. "The doors are unlocked. All is ready."

"Will you come with me, my lord? I will explain."

"Ah, the campaign continues?"

"It does."

She led him to the back. Another woman worked in the kitchen. In one corner she had trays of small, rounded loaves laid out and she stood at the stove, stirring something that smelled wonderful. "Oyster stew today," she told Lady Hope.

She sniffed appreciatively. "I'm sure it will be well received." She led on, taking a narrow stair at the back to a sparse bedroom upstairs. A wide door on the far wall looked out of place, until Tensford realized it was a pass door that connected this building to the next.

They went through, to a room set up as a parlor, but with a cot in the corner. Lady Hope went to the window and adjusted the drapes, leaving an opening down the middle.

"Come and look," she beckoned.

An alley lay below and the back door to the bakery

kitchen. The half door had been left open at the top and steam and the smell of the stew drifted out.

"Now, stand back, please. Just a step or two. They will not come if they think they are being watched. Can you still see the back door?"

He nodded, mystified.

"Good. Stay there and watch. We'll wait. Let me know if you see anyone down there."

She settled into a nearby chair. "You've been scarce these last days, sir. Have you been on the hunt for Lady X?"

"I have."

She stilled. "Did you find her?"

"Almost. I am very close."

She pressed her lips together.

"You still disapprove."

"I've been reading back over her sheets. I believe she overreacted to the stories that were going around about you and your family and I wondered why. To sell more papers? To create a scandal? Was she trying to say something to the *ton* without saying it directly?"

"And what did you conclude?"

"Nothing absolute, but I did see a hint of a pattern. She seems to react strongly to any idea of a woman in peril or a girl neglected, or one pushed into marriage by her family."

It hit him like a bullet, the crux of what she was saying. "You think she reacted strongly to the stories of me neglecting or abusing the women in my family, because she is suffering a similar situation?"

She lifted a shoulder. "How can we know for sure? But I think it is a possibility."

His mind began to churn out scenarios. Was Lady X writing her scandal sheet for money? For revenge? As a small, secret rebellion?

So many emotions. Empathy. Anger. Frustration. But when he looked at Lady Hope he felt nothing but wonder.

"All these years, she's been publishing. They all hang on her words. Yet no one noticed? No one thought to look. Until you."

She was . . . he didn't even know how to describe it. She was so different, so much more than any other woman he'd even known.

He took a step toward her—but movement in the alley below caught his eye. He turned.

"Someone is below."

She moved to his side. "Be sure to stay back out of sight."

A stack of crates sat down there, between their spot and the bakery door. A young girl had crept out from behind it.

"She must have been there all this time," he said.

"She's being careful. The crates are purposeful. They create a sheltered spot, one that cannot be seen from the street."

The girl crept to the bakery door and peeked over the edge of the half door. She was young. Five years? Six? Thin and wearing a dirty smock. She scratched at the door and held something up. It looked like a coin.

The woman in the kitchen came at once. She carried one of the round loaves. It had been hollowed into a bowl and was filled with the stew. She gave it to the girl, who turned and beckoned.

An even smaller child crept out, hurrying to take the bowl. The woman brought another and the pair retreated again, going to their sheltered spot to eat.

"The woman didn't take the coin."

"It's not a coin. It's a token." Lady Hope looked as serious as he'd ever seen her. "It's a very great secret we trust you with, my lord. A program begun by Hestia Wright, of Half Moon

House, several years ago. The children may come at any time the bakery is open. They present their token—it has a swan on it, for *Le Cygne*—and they are fed. No questions asked."

Below, another figure had turned into the alley. A boy. A bit older. His feet were bare. He kept to the shadows, presented his token and bolted his bowl right there at the door, his shoulders hunched while he ate. Glancing over at the girls, he exchanged wary nods with the eldest and slunk back the way he'd come.

"The children make the choices and distribute the tokens. They must keep the secret, not rush the bakery or share the information with any who would come to make trouble or harass Madame out of misery or spite."

"They are given responsibility for the continuation of the program," he said, understanding.

"They have done very well. Incidents have been few. The Duchess of Aldmere, working with Hestia Wright, expanded the idea, founding another similar spot in Wapping. Gradually, she recruited other like-minded ladies in the *ton*, so that the program is beginning to spread across the city. The young lady I wished to tell you about today learned of it from her mother. They've opened the newest spot, out of a chop house near Lincolns Inn Fields."

He was mulling it all over. "The tokens are brilliant. And the idea that they must protect the program. It unites them and makes them a part of it. It's all so . . ." He shook his head. "Vast. So much bigger than my poor efforts. The sheer enormity of it—it boggles the mind." He shook his head. "Started by a former courtesan and continued by the attention and generosity of Society ladies—and no one has the least notion of it."

He bowed his head. The turmoil inside of him grew larger and darker and so much more difficult to resist. "I don't wish for you to continue your campaign," he said roughly.

"No?" She sounded startled.

"No. You've won. You've convinced me. There are good and decent women in all levels of Society. People willing to work hard and care for family and others, too."

His pulse thundered. His temple throbbed. He lifted his head and stared at her. "I am convinced—and I know what I am supposed to do now. I should be asking you to introduce me to one or two or more of these paragons. Because I assume they have the appropriate requirements—single status and a good deal of money. Am I right?"

She exhaled a long breath and said nothing.

"How am I supposed to ask such a thing?" he demanded.

"They are simple words." Her eyes glittered, sharp and bright. "Just ask."

"I cannot. And you know why."

Her cheeks were glowing.

Only the soft, quick sound of their breathing lived in the quiet of the room. Her pulse fluttered at her throat.

He pulled in a ragged breath. His skin had gone too tight. He felt feverish and furious and bursting with anger and thwarted desire. "I don't want some mythically kind girl with a bulging dowry, Hope. I want you."

In her face he saw the same sort of hope and pain and need that were tearing him apart inside.

He stepped close. He touched her waist and then allowed his hand to continue on, settling into the beckoning curve of the small of her back.

Her face turned up. She looked fierce and proud and yearning—and he knew she would not be the one to initiate this kiss.

He shouldn't.

But he did.

And it was glorious and lovely and *right*. She melted beneath him and they flowed together, two rivers of desire joining into one in a confluence of rough, raw emotion.

It took almost no time to coax her mouth to open to his. Her hands clutched his shoulders, moved behind his neck.

Duty and responsibility be damned. He was just a man, reveling in heat, tasting the velvet sweetness of his woman, fitting his rising cock into her welcoming curves.

He buried his face into the arch of her throat, touched his tongue to the beat of her racing pulse.

He wanted to bare her creamy skin.

He wanted to tug her over to that cot, toss up her skirts and make them both mad with desire.

He wanted to take her home to Greystone and never let her go.

But he could not.

So he lifted his head.

Without words, she protested.

But he slid his hands to her shoulders and kissed her temple. "We should go."

They held each other up a moment. When he was finally sure he could walk without staggering or snatching her back, he huffed out a breath and stepped away.

Silently, they watched each other over across a stretch of floor that might as well have been an ocean.

At last, she nodded. Neither spoke as they retraced their steps. She waved goodbye to the Madame and her assistant. He helped her into the curricle.

They drove, swaddled inside a thick silence.

"I'm engaged to take dinner with my family and a guest this evening," she said as they pulled up before her brother's house. "Later we will be attending the Montbarrow's party. Several young ladies who might be flattered by your attentions will be there. Miss Nichols will be glad to introduce you to them. But if you find you have . . . something you'd rather say to me . . ." She faltered, took a deep breath, then continued. "I will make sure to be in Lady Montbarrow's parlor on the second floor, at the top of the stairs, at half past ten."

He nodded.

A footman emerged to help her down. She stood on the pavement, watching him gravely. "Will you come? I hope you will come."

"Then I will," he said roughly.

She turned and preceded the servant into the house.

Tensford drove away, knowing that she'd taken the best part of him with her.

CHAPTER 8

We are a civilized lot, ladies and gentlemen, and when we make a mistake, we must be prepared to admit the truth of it, and to make amends . . .
    --Whispers from Lady X

STERNE HAD ALREADY DRESSED for the evening, so his valet was free to attend to Tensford. He might have enjoyed the process, having forgotten what a luxury it was to allow someone else to press his clothes, shave him and tie him into an elegant, complicated cravat, but he was far too distracted.

It was an impossible decision.

How could he choose his own happiness over the duty he owed to his estate, his people? It was not the way a gentleman behaved.

Feeling like a fraud, he walked stiff-legged down the stairs. It felt wrong, somehow, that his shining outside did not reflect the bleak, bleeding despair he felt on the inside.

Laughter drifted from the parlor. It was to be a dinner party, the valet had told him. Tensford wished fervently that he hadn't agreed to attend. He was torn, and too, he was troubled by a nagging feeling, a thought that he'd forgotten something, or missed something important. He wanted only to hide and brood, and somehow decide if he could make that appointment with Lady Hope at Montbarrow's tonight.

How could he?

How could he not?

With a shake of his head, he bade the footman not to open the parlor doors. Not just yet. He stood a moment, looking around, letting the peace of the place sink in.

Barrett's uncle's house was small, but quite . . . splendid. The colors were warm and the lighting soft and inviting. The rug appeared worn, but everything looked scrubbed and polished and well cared for. Lady Hope's earlier words echoed in his head. *We are fortunate, all of us who know the comfort of good smells, a warm welcome and a full belly.*

He nodded and the footman opened the door. Tensford stepped into the parlor, and relaxed a little. It was that sort of atmosphere. The swish of silk and satin was the same, the gleam of jewels and smiles were as one would find at a *ton* gathering. But the crowd was small, and seemed intimate. Conversations flowed with familiar ease. There was nothing frantic or artificial about the feeling in the room.

"There you are." Sterne handed him a drink. "Let me show you around and introduce you to a few people."

In normal circumstances Tensford would have been thrilled to be there. More than a few people there had interest in the sciences, naturally. Lady Hargrove was there. She was kind, as was most everyone else. Yet Tensford could scarcely concentrate. He could not think past the ache in his chest and that niggle in his brain.

Then Barrett was back. "Come," he said. "Let's go pay respects to my aunt and uncle."

Mr. John Sterne was friendly, as always, and his wife

welcoming.

"Barrett says you intend to sell that fossilized sea urchin of yours, the one embedded in the round stone."

"I am considering it, sir."

"A fine piece. Unique. I'd be interested, of course. Give you a fair price, too. But you have a fine mind for the science yourself, Tensford. Why not keep the piece and let it be the start of your own collection?"

"I would like to. I'll think about your advice, sir."

"I know what you are thinking," Barrett said after his aunt and uncle moved on. "You're thinking you'll keep that piece if you marry the Irish merchant's daughter."

"I might as well get something above the forty thousand, for that will all go to Greystone."

"She's the worst prospect yet."

"She's the only prospect so far."

"Still, you cannot marry her." He shuddered. "I met her last night, out with your mother. She's glittery, I give you, but hard underneath."

"I have more than just myself to consider," he said irritably. "But perhaps Lady Hope will come up with a suitable candidate."

"That's just it. I think you should consider Lady Hope."

Tensford closed his eyes.

"It's why I invited you here tonight. I wanted to tell you more about my uncle."

"What about him?"

"He was never meant to marry my aunt, you know. The family had picked out his bride."

"Who?"

"My mother."

"Your mother?" Tensford said, shocked. "No offense meant, Sterne, but your mother is nothing like your aunt. She's so . . . formal."

"And cold. You can say it. And I'll add dull to the stack. But she had the money the family wished to use to ease Uncle John's fate as a second son."

"What happened?"

"They were not suited. She was happier with my father, as heir to the title and as a man closer to her in disposition. Uncle John loved another. And my aunt loved him. The family wasn't happy, but they married in spite of the objections. Their road has not always been easy. They don't have the funds my parents do, but they've done well for themselves."

"Yes," he agreed, looking around.

"They've created a home. A place of warmth and caring."

"And I know they've been generous in sharing it with you, my friend."

"Thank God, they have. It wins hands down over the sterile atmosphere of my own home, as you know. So you see, their marriage affected more than just their own lives. They've touched so many. Created a community," he said, gesturing around.

Understanding began to dawn as Sterne continued.

"In my mind, your Greystone has been like my parent's house. Grand, but cold. No heart to the place. Empty of joy and warmth and welcome and the things that truly make a home. And I know you want a home, Tensford, not just a restored house. God knows, you deserve to finally have one."

He shook his head.

"It's one thing if you marry Miss McNamara knowing that she does not care for you. But remember, too, that when you choose a bride, you must bring her home to Greystone. She will be in charge of the house and your servants and in constant contact with the people on your land. She will raise your children." Sterne frowned at him. "Will she have a care for any of that?"

Tensford stared.

"One more thing. I think you need to remember that your people care for you, just as you care for them. Do you think they would ask you to make this sacrifice? To resign yourself to a lifetime of misery married to the wrong woman, for their sake?"

He didn't know the answer.

"Dinner is ready," the butler intoned at the doorway.

Woodenly, Tensford followed the party to the dining room. He took his seat—and proceeded to act as history's worst dinner guest.

He ate nothing. He spoke to neither of the ladies on either side of him. He merely stared into his wine and contemplated the largest decision of his life.

Was his heart agreeing with Barrett because it was what he wished to hear? Because he did want Lady Hope Brightley with a passion bordering on madness. He wanted her wit and her charm and her kisses. Her wanted her mornings and her nights and every hour from here to eternity. He went a little mad every time he thought of her choosing, marrying, someone else.

His heart kept whispering that Barrett was right, so he let his brain do as it wished and compare the choices that lay before him.

A union made for money. Greystone Park with a new roof, restored outbuildings, a set future, but no soul. A loveless marriage at the center of it. This would be their fate if he took Miss McNamara as his bride, or even some yet-to-be-met candidate that Lady Hope brought to him.

But Lady Hope. His head couldn't keep up with the images he finally allowed himself to conjure. Her laughter ringing through the house. Her compassion a balm to his people. It would be a life of hard work, but she would be there by his side. It was so easy to imagine his servants loving her as he did, to picture her listening to their woes, carrying baskets to the sick, attending the fairs, becoming a part of their community.

Laughter at Greystone. Hope. Hard work.

Love.

Abruptly, he stood. What time was it? He didn't care. He had to find her and tell her. Ask her to share his life. "Please excuse me," he said to the staring tableful of guests. "I suddenly realized . . . recalled . . . something extremely urgent."

Mrs. Sterne's eyes softened. "Of course, dear boy."

"Go on, then." Mr. Sterne shooed him.

Tensford raced out. He waited impatiently for his cloak, trying to recall where the nearest hack stand would be. He raced down the front steps—and skidded to a halt when a boy stepped out of the shadows into his path.

Lady X's messenger boy.

"My mistress says she'll meet you—if you promise not to unmask her to the world."

Tensford shook his head.

The boy looked upset. "She says as she feels like she owes it to you to talk, but if you won't promise, then I cannot tell you where to meet her."

"No, that isn't it." Lord, he was a lovesick fool, but he couldn't summon any further desire for revenge or confrontation. "Tell your employer . . ." He thought of Lady Hope's defense of him, her desire to repay him for reviving Lady X's interest. He thought of the empathy that she'd shown the anonymous lady. "Tell your mistress that if ever she needs a champion, or help of any kind, then she may call on Lord Tender."

He left the surprised boy behind and ran forward to hail a hack.

CHAPTER 9

I hear from several sources that Lord Tender has been running amuck again, acting oddly at Mr. Sterne's dinner party and assorted other gatherings. But as he's held up so well under my interference and appears to perhaps be thriving under the influence of certain others . . . we must forgive him.

--Whispers from Lady X

"Lord Bardham," Hope said with a sigh. "I am just on my way to speak with Miss Nichols."

"Where is your gallant suitor, Lady Hope?" Bardham asked with a sneer. "I hear he has a bigger fish on his line these days. Has he deserted you?"

"If you speak of Lord Tensford, I have not seen him this evening." A wicked idea occurred to her. "But if you speak of Miss McNamara, I could hardly be angry if he has decided to pursue her. Who could compete?"

"With a merchant's daughter?" he scoffed.

"A pretty merchant's daughter who brings forty thousand pounds. I could hardly begrudge him for being interested."

"Forty . . . thousand?" he whispered.

"Yes. I heard Lady Tensford say so, to one of her friends. I daresay they hope it doesn't get around right away or the girl will be swamped."

"That's her, is it not?" Bardham asked. "By the French doors?"

She looked. "I believe so."

"Tensford is not there," he reflected.

"No doubt he'll be here soon enough. Lord Bardham?"

But the coarse, predictable man was already drifting away. Hope moved on, shaking her head, until she reached Miss Nichols.

"How do I look?" she asked her friend, nervously smoothing her skirts.

"Stunning. And frightened half to death." Miss Nichols patted her arm. "Calm down. All will go well."

"I hope so. But I cannot be sure."

"I can. I've seen how he looks at you."

"He might be angry." It was just one of the risks she'd taken.

"He might. But would you change anything you've done?"

"No." She thought about it. "No. It's better this way."

"Then head up there. He'll be here soon." Laughing, she gave Hope a push. "And don't come down until you've got him."

Hope started to go, but paused as several footmen entered, carrying trays of canapés. "Lobster patties," she said. "Save some for me? They might end up being my only consolation."

"You can serve them at your wedding," Miss Nichols told her. "Now go on."

* * *

TENSFORD WAS STRIDING into the Montbarrow's party when it hit him.

He saw the butler fussing, overseeing the comings and goings of a fleet of footmen, all carrying trays of food and drinks. And he knew what had been nagging at him. Suddenly his mind flashed back to the afternoon at *Le Cygne*.

He remembered what Madame Hobert had said. *Everything is fine, yes?* And then, *Lady Hope and her friends are always welcome, and they do not pay here.*

Why not? Why would the Madame be so grateful?

A familiar laugh rang out and he caught sight of his mother and Miss McNamara. Bardham was standing before them, acting the peacock. And that pulled forth another niggling thread. Two thousand pounds for her dowry, that's what Hope had told him. And Bardham had been chasing her for it? Or was he chasing her in spite of it? Such a sum might cover the man's debts, but it wouldn't set him up for the rest of his life—and it wasn't like Bardham to choose a smart, pretty girl over his life's ease.

Was that it? Did she have other money, that only Bardham, as her family's friend, might know about? Did Madame Hobert show such gratitude because Lady Hope was a benefactress of Madame's program, feeding the children?

He thought of what Hope had said about the young woman who had opened the newest arm of the project. Was it her? Had she been introducing him to her qualities and concerns, rather than those of anonymous ladies of the *ton*? But then, what of the other one? The letter writer? Had that been her, too?

But that would mean . . .

He stared up the stairs, but then turned and stalked resolutely into the crowd. He looked around wildly—there. He approached Lady Kincade and bowed.

"Lord Tensford," Hope's sister-in-law said sourly.

"How nice to see you again, my lady. I understand you had guests to dinner tonight."

"Guest," she corrected. "Weatherby."

"Ah, of the Stud Book family?"

"Yes. Tiresome, to be so consumed with horses. I vow, we would have been here ages ago, had Hope not quizzed the man on generations of horseflesh. As if one must know all of that history before buying a mount for a young girl. But I suppose she'll write it all in one those tomes she sends her sister."

He straightened. "You mean letters to her sister?"

"Yes. She's lucky her brother can frank them, thick as they are," she grumbled. "Nothing but dresses and horses."

"Letters to her *lame* sister?" he asked tightly.

"Have they another?" the countess asked snidely. "If they do, I remain unaware."

"Yes. Thank you, Lady Kincade." His mind was racing. "Good evening."

He turned on his heel without waiting for a response and nearly collided with a footman carrying a tray.

A tray of lobster patties. He froze for a moment, then reached out and deftly took the platter from the startled servant. "I'll return the tray, sir, do not worry." He left the ballroom and took the stairs, two at a time.

* * *

THE PARLOR DOOR BURST OPEN. Hope nearly burst out of her skin.

"Lord Tensford! Here you are," she said pedantically. Why did he carry a silver serving tray?

"Here *we* are," he corrected. He looked around. "But are there no other young ladies? No one for me to meet?"

"Well, I—"

"Never mind," he interrupted. "We'll enjoy these before we go to make the introductions." He approached her and held out the tray.

"Lobster patties," she said weakly. Her stomach was aflutter. She couldn't eat a bite.

"Yes. We never did share any, that first night. The night we met. We spoke of sharing the last lobster patty—and other things. Do you remember?"

Oh, she remembered.

"In any case, I have these. And a question. I'll trade you for the answer."

"Of course." He was in a strange mood. How was she going to explain if he would not stop going on about lobster patties?

"Mmm." He held the tray beneath her nose. "Don't they smell wonderful? But wait—that is not my question. I was just wondering about the tokens you mentioned earlier. The new tokens for the chophouse, they won't have a swan on them, I wouldn't think. What image is carved on the new tokens?"

"A meat cleaver," she said absently, watching him move the tray before her. She had to bring this conversation around.

"Why did you choose a meat cleaver?"

"It fit the chophouse and I thought the boys would like it bett—" She stopped suddenly and looked up at him. "Wait." She pushed the tray away. "You know!"

"I do know."

"But, how?" And how did he feel about it? She was in a panic. His expression was so . . . bland. Clutching her fists, she lifted her chin and tried to calm her racing heart. "I have questions of my own," she said finally.

"Ah, but what will you trade for answers?"

She drew a deep breath. "Pots and pots of money."

He winced. "That's what I thought it would be."

She searched his face. "I am sorry for deceiving you. But do you understand? Why I did . . . everything?"

"I think I do. You said it yourself. I had no liking for being rejected because of my lack of funds. Nor do you wish to be courted for your possession of them. But how? How is it not widely known?"

"I made my brother promise not to tell. I told him he owed it to me, after leaving me to care for our mother alone while she suffered and withered away, so slowly."

"Then your father left you more than the two thousand?"

"No. That was my dowry. But my Aunt Margaret died before my mother, her sister. Her husband was a nabob and had made a fortune in the East. They had no children and we had been close. She left it all to me. I was in the midst of nursing my mother and barely registered it at first. But afterwards, I forced him to promise. No one knows except the family."

"And Bardham, one assumes."

She made a face. "Not even Catherine knows the true extent of it." She grinned. "And in any case, I think that tonight, I dealt with Bardham at last."

"How?"

"I sent him off after Miss McNamara and her forty thousand pounds."

He laughed. "They will be perfect for each other."

"I'm sorry for putting you through so much, but I had to know . . . I wanted to be chosen . . ."

"For yourself," he said, taking her hands.

"And it was important that you should know, too. We both deserved to know we chose each other." She sighed—but then tossed her head. "But I don't care, I want—"

"No! Throw that thought right out of your head. I did. I made my choice tonight at the Sterne's dinner party. When I thought you had no more than your dowry. Before I suspected the rest of it. Barrett invited me because he wanted to make a point and I listened. To him, and to my heart, at last. I imagined the bride I would bring back to Greystone and I knew it couldn't ever be anyone but you."

He took her hand. "I've thought for so long that all that Greystone needed was money. But Barrett made me realize —there was money at Greystone once, before my father died —and yet it was never really a home, not even then. What Greystone needs, what I need—is something that we've never had. It needs you. I need you. I need your heart, your love. It's the only thing that will make it a home—a life—worth living."

She blinked back tears, but he was grinning now. "And if you need confirmation, then ask anyone at the Sterne's dinner. I made an ass of myself, running out in the middle of the fish course."

"Truly?"

"I swear it. It wasn't until I arrived here that I put it all together. I saw the butler worrying over the food—and I remembered what Madame said yesterday, about never allowing you to pay."

She groaned and laughed. "I thought I would sink beneath the table when she said it, but you never seemed to connect her words with what I had to show you, so I just moved forward."

"Yes, I was slow. But I was learning about you, even if I did think you were speaking of some other young lady." He sighed. "And then I saw Bardham skulking around Miss McNamara and it all just clicked into place."

He sighed. "I shouldn't ask. I have nothing to give you except . . . me. These hands, a drafty, leaking estate, hard work aplenty—but we will do it together, Hope, and you will have my heart—and all of my love."

"I was hoping for a few other things."

"Anything," he vowed. "Anything I can give you, I will."

"A dance," she whispered. "A jaunt into dangerous territory . . ."

He remembered. That first night. "And bliss," he finished.

And she was in his arms and the kiss lasted quite a long while, as they shared their happiness, forgiveness and relief. They planned a lifetime of love with heat and passion instead of words. They kissed and touched and whispered together until a knock sounded on the door.

"You've been in there long enough," Miss Nichols said through the panel. "The countess is looking for you."

They went out then and followed her friend downstairs, still with eyes only for each other.

But Tensford's mind had turned to their future. "We can get the large saws we need for the mill and perhaps the steam engine. It may be, if we can turn enough profit, that we will need only to cut part of the forest acreage."

She pulled him to a stop at the bottom of the stairs. "No. We will not cut down even one tree. I have enough to do all that we could wish at Greystone."

He frowned. "Hope—just how much does pots and pots of money work out to be?"

"A lot. Far more than Miss McNamara's paltry forty thousand."

He blinked. Then stumbled back a step to sit upon a nearby bench.

She followed and perched upon his knee. "We'll have lobster patties every day!" she cried, throwing an arm high.

"And bliss every night," he murmured, pulling her down.

And so they kissed again, while the footmen snickered and inside, the *ton* danced on.

ABOUT THE AUTHOR

USA Today Bestselling author Deb Marlowe adores History, England and Men in Boots. Clearly she was destined to write Historical Romance.

A Golden Heart winner and Rita nominee, Deb writes Regency Romance and Young Adult Fantasy Adventure.

A proud geek, history buff and story addict, she loves to talk with readers! Find her discussing books, movies, TV, recipes from Deb Marlowe's Regency Kitchen and her infamous Men in Boots on Facebook, Twitter, Instagram, and Pinterest.

Connect with Deb
www.DebMarlowe.com
Deb@DebMarlowe.com

ALSO BY DEB MARLOWE

A Series of Unconventional Courtships

Love Me, Lord Tender

Nothing But a Rakehell

Kiss Me, Lady, One More Time

The Half Moon House Series

The Novels

The Love List

The Leading Lady

The Lady's Legacy

The Lady's Lover

The Novellas

An Unexpected Encounter

A Slight Miscalculation

A Waltz in the Park

Liberty and the Pursuit of Happiness

Beyond a Reasonable Duke

Lady, It's Cold Outside

The Earl's Hired Bride

The Castle Keyvnor Pixies

Lady Tamsyn and the Pixie's Curse

Lord Locryn and the Pixie's Kiss

9 781737 620938